Kindred Spirits

Prequel Short Stories to The Sapphire Necklace

C.A. Varian

Contents

Hazel's Story

Chapter One
Moving Forward

Sitting alone at Cafe du Monde, enjoying a hot cup of coffee and an extremely messy beignet, Hazel Watson flipped through the apartment rental apps in search of a new apartment. She had finished law school only a few weeks prior, had been promised a full-time position as a public defender for the City of New Orleans, and now needed to move into her own place like a grown-up. She groaned in protest at the thought of it.

After nearly seven years in a dorm room with a roommate, she was excited to live alone, but she was not thrilled about being solely responsible for the bills and housework, which she was infamously bad at handling. The idea that all lawyers were rich, a lie she'd been fed when she was young, was not true. Having just started out in her field, she wasn't even sure how she would make rent.

She would have probably had a much easier time finding a place to live in other towns, smaller towns, but she wanted to stay in New Orleans, which was not an inexpensive endeavor. Having attended law school in New Orleans, she had stayed to build a life there, although she, being an introvert, had very few friends. Friends or not, she had grown to love so much about the city. Also, being a bit estranged from her father, she preferred to stay as far away from New Mexico as she could. Sighing and clicking on another site, when she overheard an interesting conversation start up at the table next to her. Keeping her face in her phone so she could appear to be busy, she focused in on the conversation between the two young women sitting to her right.

"Any luck finding a place?" asked one girl, who sported a short, purple pixie cut and baggy clothes. She appeared to be of college age.

"Not quite," responded her friend, who was dressed in all black, with lipstick to match. "I looked at one place yesterday, but it won't work out."

The girl in black looked troubled, but more troubled than she should have been because of a failed housing search. Instead, Hazel thought, she appeared to be traumatized. She held her arms around herself as her eyes scanned the room.

"What happened?" Her friend scooted her chair closer.

The girl in the all black attire hesitated, but just for a moment.

"Something was in that house," she whispered, peering around to make sure no one was listening. "I should have known when the realtor stayed in the corridor instead of coming inside with me. The apartment was small but nice. But the minute I walked in the door the television turned on by itself, and the remote flew across the room."

Her friend giggled, which caused the goth girl to appear as though she felt attacked. Her eyebrows furrowed as she looked towards the ground, fingers fumbling with the hem of her top, as though believing in such things embarrassed her enough to not be able to look her friend in the eye.

"I'm not making it up!" She quickly pushed her chair away from the table. But before she could storm off, her friend reached across the table and grabbed her hand.

"Okay, I'm sorry. I believe you. If you need a place to stay for now, you can always sleep on my couch. I'm sure something will open up for you."

The girl in all black quickly nodded her head before scooting her chair back to the table.

Deciding to interrupt the conversation, Hazel turned her body towards the two friends.

"Excuse me."

Both girls looked at her, startled, jumping when her voice interrupted their moment.

"I'm sorry to interrupt, but I kind of overheard part of your conversation. I think I heard you say that there may be a decent apartment available, one that you didn't want to rent?"

"Yes," responded the goth girl. "It was too... um... noisy."

Hazel realized the girl was minimizing her hypothesis of the apartment being haunted, but Hazel played along.

"That's okay. I just really need a place to move into that I can afford. I just finished law school, so I can't stay in the dorms. Would you be okay with giving me the address or the contact information for the realtor who is renting it?"

"Uh, sure." The girl in all black pulled a notepad out of her bag and began writing on it before handing it over to Hazel.

Hazel took the slip of paper and examined it. The handwriting was difficult to understand, not much more than a scribbled mess, probably because the girl was still startled by what she'd experienced in the apartment. In looking at the scribbled words on the page, Hazel saw a realtor's name and the address for the apartment. She took a moment to look up directions to the complex on her phone, which got her excited because the apartment appeared to be close to her office. Her excitement quickly turned into uneasiness, however, because she didn't know what she would find when she went to the apartment to look at it. Hazel flashed a grateful smile.

"Thank you so much. I really owe you one."

"Don't thank me yet," murmured the still-traumatized girl.

Nodding her head and giving a small wave, Hazel pocketed the sheet of paper and made her way to the exit.

When she got to her car, she quickly pulled the sheet of paper back out of her bag and dialed the phone number for the realtor. She needed a place to live as soon as possible, so she couldn't risk someone else snagging it. To Hazel's delight, the realtor, a woman named Samantha Bourgeois, answered the call.

"Bourgeois Realty," said the woman on the other end of the line.

Hazel hesitated, twisting in her chair.

"Hi! I heard you had an apartment for rent on Loyola Avenue. I was calling to see if it's still available."

The realtor was quiet for a moment, making Hazel's heart sink at the idea that the apartment may no longer be available.

Hazel cleared her throat, pulling the realtor back into their conversation.

"Sorry. I do have a vacant apartment. However, I no longer have it listed, because it's had some... um... problems. You surprised me by asking about it, because I wasn't sure how you had heard about it."

"Oh, I see. I don't mind a bit of noise, Ms. Bourgeois. I just really need to find a place in my budget and near the courthouse. I must move within the next few weeks. Is there any way I can look at it?"

The realtor fell silent once again, but only briefly.

"It'll probably be a waste of both of our time, but I can make it happen if you insist on seeing it."

The excitement Hazel had felt earlier flooded back.

"Yes! That would be great!"

Hazel was thrilled about the apartment because it was close to her office, and the rent was affordable, especially for New Orleans. Noisy neighbors, boisterous poltergeists, it didn't matter. She had an appointment scheduled to see the place, and she was feeling hopeful.

Chapter Two
The Occupied Apartment

On the following day, Hazel met the realtor, Ms. Samantha Bourgeois, outside of the Loyola Avenue apartment complex. The apartment building was clearly old, but the style reminded her of Roman architecture. The windows across the bottom level were arched. Although the building was dark brick, there were several detailed additions in a lighter beige color to give the building some contrast. It was situated right next to Tulane Medical Center.

Making their way into the building, Hazel gazed around at the architectural details that had been maintained since the building's inception. Although the building was designed with a modern aesthetic in mind, with lots of blacks, whites, and metal, it still held some of that historical New Orleans charm.

"It's quite nice," she said, turning to look at the realtor.

"Oh, yes. The building dates to over one hundred years ago, but they tried to maintain some of its original design when adding the new modern touches."

"I like it. What floor are we going to?"

"We're going to the third floor."

Ms. Bourgeois led their way to the shiny gold elevators.

Heading up in the elevator, Hazel felt her nerves intensify, and her heart started to pound. She wasn't afraid of spirits, since she had communicated with them since she was born, but she was nervous that the spirit in the apartment would be too much for her to deal with. Getting out of the elevator and walking to the door for apartment 301, she took a deep breath and let it out slowly, and then walked inside. As the goth girl had mentioned, the realtor stayed in the corridor.

"Look around. I'll wait here and make some phone calls. Let me know if you have questions."

Hazel nodded in acknowledgement and then turned to face the room. She walked into an open concept living and kitchen area. The main living space was small, but enough for just her. Feeling a sudden chill, Hazel wrapped her arms around her chest, rubbing her arms to warm them.

She immediately felt tension, so thick she could cut it with a knife. As soon as she crossed from the kitchen into the living room, the television turned on by itself, the remote control flew from the sofa onto the floor, and the drapes flew closed over the windows, throwing the space into darkness. Hazel yelped, but then scanned the room, trying to find the source of the haunting. She couldn't see a spirit, but that didn't mean there wasn't one present. It was simply not revealing itself. Slowly, Hazel walked over and turned off the television, but before she could walk away it turned back on, and the channels switched until they landed on a channel that only played true crime murder mysteries. Gingerly, she backed up and sat down on the sofa.

"You're not scaring me," she whispered, looking around for some sign of a presence. "You might as well show yourself."

Within a matter of seconds, another woman, probably in her early twenties, manifested in a large chair across from her. The first thing that caught Hazel's attention was the spirit's fiery red hair. Although she was a spirit, she was strong enough to manifest herself into an almost solid form. The woman looked at Hazel with amusement.

"I can see you and I can hear you. What are you doing here?"

"This is my apartment, doll," the spirit replied. "So, what are *you* doing here?"

Hazel paused for a moment to plan her words carefully.

"You know that you're..." Hazel trailed off.

"Dead? Yes, love. I know that. Regardless, this is still my place," the red-headed spirit responded with a dismissive wave of her hand.

"What's your name?"

"Candy. Now please let that realtor know my apartment is not for rent and go on your way."

Hazel felt her cortisol levels rise, but Candy looked unfazed.

"I'm sorry, Candy, but I can't do that. If it isn't me who moves in, it'll be someone else. If we could learn to live together, then you would at least have someone to talk to, unless you're willing to cross over, but they will not stop looking for a renter."

Candy rolled her eyes, and Hazel felt even more uncomfortable. She was an introvert to a fault. Therefore, she didn't converse with people much, aside from the spirits who came to her for help. But a spirit with an attitude problem... That was not something she knew how to handle.

"I'm not crossing over, or whatever you call it. I'm happy enough where I am." Candy's voice got higher as her rant progressed.

"I don't understand. Don't you want to see what lies beyond?"

"No way, doll. There's still a party in this world and I don't intend to leave it just because some bastard stabbed me in the back."

Candy seemed nonchalant but Hazel felt sorry for her. How horrible it must have been to have her life taken from her at such a young age. Candy couldn't have been more than twenty-five years old. Hazel's heart went out to her. Suddenly, she felt a need to live in the apartment with Candy. Although she didn't make friends easily and had intended to cross over the apartment's resident spirit once she moved in, she now felt the need to be there for her. Even though Candy seemed happy in her afterlife, Hazel suspected it was all a façade.

"I'm really sorry that happened to you,"

Hazel chanced a sympathetic smile.

The realtor opened the door, peeking her head in, and Hazel jumped.

"Are you alright, Hazel? I'm still making phone calls but wanted to make sure you didn't need any help," Ms. Bourgeois asked.

"No. I'm fine," responded Hazel. "I'm just trying to get a feel for the place."

"Oh, okay. I'll be right out here if you need me."

Nodding quickly, Hazel stood up from the sofa, appearing to be looking around the apartment again. This time, however, the spirit of Candy stood up and followed her.

"So, do you really think they won't stop showing the apartment until they find a tenant?"

"You can't pay rent anymore, and they don't know you're still here, so yes, I believe that. It's me or someone else."

As Candy pacing aimlessly around the room, she pondered Hazel's response. Hazel watched her, secretly hoping Candy wouldn't object to her moving into the apartment, because she really liked the space and the price.

"If you didn't move in... I could end up with someone much worse. I guess I really don't have a choice, because I'm not going anywhere."

"Uh, thanks..."

Hazel hoped she was more than a level above what Candy considered to be "much worse" but didn't dwell too far on the comment.

"I guess I understand why you don't want to cross over, but I still hope you'll give it some thought. There isn't much for you on this side of the veil... but I'm sure we can become great friends if not. I will support you either way."

"Thanks, love."

Candy threw an icy arm over Hazel's shoulder. The cold of Candy's arm jolted Hazel, and she was surprised by how solid it felt. Then, although she was nervous, she could feel Candy sending comforting energy into her body, and she knew that living with Candy was where she belonged.

Chapter Three
Uncomfortable Crushes

Moving day came rather quickly, which was a relief to Hazel. Although she knew the apartment came with a resident ghost, she felt a connection to Candy, even though they seemed so different. It was almost like they were kindred spirits, and Hazel looked forward to learning why she was so drawn to the spirit of a woman who she never knew. She'd never had many friends, but Candy was different.

The apartment came with several furnishings, including a television and stand, but Hazel enlisted the help of her college friend and local police officer, Tate Cormier, to do the heavy lifting. They had always had a flirty friendship, although it never progressed beyond that. Hazel knew she wanted more, but her life felt too complicated to get into a relationship. Plus, she didn't know if he wanted the same thing.

Pacing her dorm room floor, Hazel did one last sweep to make sure she packed all her belongings and that they were all accounted for. Feeling satisfied that her packing was complete, she sent a text message to Tate, asking him to meet up with her so he could help her move.

Tate arrived at the door rather quickly and scooped Hazel up into a big bear hug. Being over six feet tall and muscular, Hazel considered all his hugs to be bear hugs. She closed her eyes while in his arms and became intoxicated by his pheromones, pulling her eyes back down to their normal position right before he let her go. *Why did he have to be so delicious?* It was torture to be near him when she couldn't be with him, at least without the chance of ruining their friendship. Tate grabbed her belongings, stacking several boxes at a time, and trudged down the hall to the stairs, only stopping once he reached her car.

"You didn't have to carry all of those at once."

This way, we only have to make a few trips." With a smirk, Tate lifted the boxes higher. "It's not too heavy."

"If you say so." The wink he gave her when she patted him on the back made her heart melt.

With both vehicles full of her worldly possessions, they were forced to drive separately to her new apartment. Although she was normally a borderline terrible driver, Hazel did her best to follow all the traffic rules, since a cop was trailing her. Tate may have been a good friend, but she still wanted to make sure to not blatantly break any rules of the road with him watching. Once they got to her new apartment, they both grabbed whatever boxes they could safely carry at once and headed to the elevator, which took them to the third floor.

"Nice place," Tate said, throwing a smile her way. She felt a flush spread across her cheeks.

"Thanks." She blushed as she pressed the button to call down the elevator.

She chewed at her nails nervously, unsure of how Candy would respond to her bringing Tate into the apartment. She hoped Candy wouldn't do anything crazy, but she didn't know her well enough to trust she wouldn't.

Upon entering the apartment, everything seemed quiet. They dropped the boxes in the kitchen and walked around the space as Hazel gave Tate a tour.

"I like it." His handsome smile remained on his face, making it difficult for Hazel to keep her face from turning red.

"Thanks! It's not much, but it's enough for me."

"It's also close to your office, which should be convenient. You won't have to brave too much traffic every day."

"Yeah. That's one of the biggest pros to taking this place. The realtor said it can be noisy here, but I'll deal with it for the price and short distance to work."

"Noisy how?" His eyebrows lowered, the look more animated than it should have been.

Hazel shrugged her shoulders. "She didn't say."

Tate didn't know about her hereditary gift, the one that allowed her to communicate with the dead, and she preferred to keep it that way. She didn't want to chance him thinking she was crazy. It was one of the fundamental things that prevented her from pursuing him, although she was too shy to make the first move, anyway. Very few people knew about her gift, other than her family and the spirits. There were some strangers who knew, but only those who believed her enough to allow her to help their dead loved ones to pass on a message before traversing the veil. Some people, however, did not believe her claims. This caused some spirits' messages to never be shared, an outcome she dreaded. Spirits weren't known for taking no for an answer, so if she could not pass along their messages, they stalked her until she did.

After a brief tour of the apartment, Hazel and Tate went back down to the parking lot so they could grab more boxes. As Tate pulled boxes out of the car, a flutter of curtains grabbed Hazel's attention. Looking up towards the window, she could see Candy looking down at them with an inquisitive look on her face. Hazel took a chance at smiling up at her, but Tate noticed.

"What are you looking at?" he asked, following her gaze back up to the window.

"Oh." Hesitating, she looked away. "I thought I saw a neighbor looking out of the window. She's gone now."

Taking his gaze away from the window, Tate looked at her again. "Well, maybe you'll have pleasant neighbors, and not those who make too much noise."

She nodded, looking back at the window skeptically.

"Yeah, hopefully."

Closing the trunk, they began their trip back up to her new apartment.

Walking into the apartment with Tate for the second time was a very different experience than the first. As soon as they opened the door, Candy popped up only a few feet ahead of them, causing Hazel to drop her box.

"Oh, shit!" She shrieked, hearing broken glass jingle within.

"I've got it." Setting down his own stack of boxes, he picked up hers, moving it out of the doorway.

"Who's the hunk?" Candy asked in a seductive tone, watching Tate like she was seducing him with her eyes.

Hazel shot a threatening glance and mouthed, "Not now!" when Tate wasn't looking.

Candy, undeterred, followed him around like a lost puppy dog, and Hazel felt incredibly uneasy. Motioning for Candy to follow her, she made her way to the bathroom. Thankfully, Candy stopped trailing Tate, and accompanied her out of the room.

"Can you please cut it out?" Hazel whispered, not wanting Tate to hear her seeming to talk to herself.

"Whatever do you mean?" Although Candy had an innocent look on her face, Hazel didn't buy it.

"Stop following him around like a bloodhound."

"Aw, why? I miss men, and this one is lovely."

Hazel rolled her eyes and then set them back on her new friend.

"I understand that, but you're making me nervous."

"Alright, I'll back off a little," Sounding defeated, Candy's shoulders slumped. "But who is he? Will he be over often?"

"He's just a friend, and probably."

"Just a friend? Oh, honey, you can do better than that." Candy waved a finger at Hazel like she was a naughty child.

"I wish," Hazel mumbled, making her way out of the bathroom and back to Tate.

She found him in the kitchen, emptying boxes and putting the contents into the cabinets.

"Oh, hey." When she walked back into the room, he grinned at her, sending heat through her cheeks. There was something about him that always made her gush like a schoolgirl.

"Hey, sorry about that."

"Don't apologize. Are you okay?"

"Oh, yeah. I just wanted to check out the cabinet space in the bathroom. So, what do you have going on in here?"

"Well, I wasn't sure where you wanted everything to go, but space is fairly limited, so I just started putting things where I would want them. Is that okay? I could move it, if you want me to."

"No, don't even think about it! I appreciate your help. Stick it wherever you want. I'll figure it out."

"Stick it wherever he wants, huh?" Candy mimicked her right near her ear, leaving her mortified. She wanted to respond, but she couldn't without looking like an insane person talking to nothing. Thankfully, Tate was digging in a box, and hadn't noticed her face. She shot a scornful look at Candy, who replied with her hands up in surrender.

"Are you hungry?" Tate asked, not seeming to notice her interaction with an invisible being.

"Starving. Got anything in mind?"

"Oh, it doesn't matter. I'll eat just about anything. How about you order for us, my treat?"

"He'll eat just about..." Candy began but stopped when Hazel shot her a death stare.

Hazel ordered from a sandwich shop she discovered only a few blocks away. As promised, Tate picked up the check, which was a relief. As she waited to start her new career with the public defender's office, she was about as broke as a joke, not that she would have much money when she did.

Since Tate worked a night shift, he left soon after eating. She was sad to see him go, but she looked forward to spending time with her new spectral friend. They were going to be stuck with each other for the foreseeable future, so they might as well get to know each other.

Chapter Four
A Life was Lost

After climbing out of the shower and throwing on a set of pajamas, Hazel found Candy laying on the sofa, watching a true crime television show. She plopped down on the sofa next to her, shivering at the chill emanating from Candy's form. Living with a spirit full-time would take some getting used to, but at least it would cool down the hellish Louisiana summers.

"Have a nice shower?" Candy asked, turning to look at Hazel with expectant eyes. "I miss being able to shower. There is so much about life that I miss."

Although Hazel nodded, she was still unsure how to respond. She felt guilty, like she had some control over what Candy was forced to be without.

"I'm sorry, Candy. I can't imagine what you've gone through."

"It is what it is, doll. No use in feeling bad about it. It's not your fault." Candy patted Hazel on the leg, the touch sending pins and needles into the limb.

"Do you want to talk about it?"

"Maybe one day, love. Let's not dredge it up today."

"Okay, well, I'm here if you change your mind. For now, I'm going to head to bed."

"Sweet dreams, roomie!" With a smile, Candy waved goodnight.

Lying in bed that night, Hazel's mind was uneasy. Sharing a home with a spirit was one thing but living in such close quarters with a murder victim was another. She didn't know how to approach Candy, how to talk to her about what happened to her. Unable to fall asleep, she grabbed her laptop off the bedside table and opened the search engine, looking for any information about the murder of a young woman by the name of Candy in New Orleans.

The search didn't take very long. A young woman named Candy Townsend was murdered in her apartment only a year prior. She was only twenty-three years old. Hazel felt her heart sink. She knew Candy was young, but she didn't realize she was *that* young. No wonder Candy didn't want to cross over. She had only just begun living her life. The article said she was stabbed to death by her boyfriend, in a jealous rage over another man, but the motive was only speculative. Hazel yearned to know the truth, but Candy made it clear she wasn't ready to talk about it, so Hazel would have to wait until she was ready.

She knew she would not sleep easily that night, but she did her best to put her thoughts about Candy's death behind her. It would do no good to dwell on something she couldn't change.

The sky was beautiful. I watched it as I grabbed my jacket and headed home from work. With fall creeping in, the night held a chill. Zipping my jacket all the way to my neck, I headed south for the three-block walk to my apartment. The leaves crunched beneath my feet as I navigated the broken pavement, being careful not to fall on my face. The building appeared deserted, not that I could expect much more at two in the morning. Hitting the three on the elevator, I readied my keys for the door.

My cortisol levels rose as the elevator chimed, announcing that I had arrived at the correct floor, but I wasn't sure where the nervousness had come from. I felt eyes on me, but I didn't see anyone lingering, so I hurried to my door, only taking a few seconds to open it. Setting my keys and purse on the kitchen table, I started to turn around and close the door, when I felt a sharp pain in my back. It hit repeatedly, like a deadly spasm, and I dropped to my knees. When I turned around to see if there was an intruder, all that laid before me was an empty doorway.

Puddles of blood circled around me, triggering me to panic. I crawled to the kitchen table as the pain erupted all around me. Reaching up to the table, I grabbed my cell phone with trembling hands, and dialed 9-1-1, before falling into unconsciousness. Bits and pieces of visions flashed through my mind like a picture reel. Men and women rushed in and out of my door. Someone lifted me and screamed to the others, but that's all I remember, all I remember, aside from the pain.

Hazel awoke from the nightmare, feeling a sinking sense of dread. Upon checking the bed for bloodstains, she sighed a breath of relief that there were none. Nightmares had been a part of her life for as long as she could remember. She couldn't even understand why she still awoke thinking that it had been an actual experience, instead of her mind playing tricks on her.

Rubbing her eyes and taking in her surroundings, it took her a moment to remember where she was. It would take some time to get used to a new place, especially a place that was quiet, unlike her dorm.

"You're awake!" squealed Candy, walking into the bedroom as though she had a corporeal form.

Hazel instantly took back the thought about living in a quiet place. Her new apartment seemed exactly like a dorm room. She sat up in her bed slightly, eyeing Candy with amusement.

"Sort of... What are you up to?"

"I was waiting for you to wake up, roomie. Have been for hours."

Too lazy to get up, Haze glanced at her cell phone to check the time.

"Candy, it's only nine in the morning. Why would I have been up hours ago?"

Shrugging, Candy flashed her a mischievous smile.

"Oh, is that all? I don't know. I haven't had to worry about clocks for ages. I don't even know what day it is."

Hazel smirked. "After finishing school, I rarely know what day it is either. Anyway, what's your plan for the day?"

"I was hoping you could tell me. I'm bored as hell, always sitting in this apartment."

"Unpacking and sleeping is all I have planned for today. I'm starting my new job next week. I need to get this place in order by then."

Pouting like a petulant child, Candy groaned. "Aw, come on. That's no fun."

Wanting to find a compromise, Hazel thought for a minute. "We can walk around the neighborhood. You can show me around. Does that sound good?" Knowing how much she needed to do, she was hopeful the brief excursion would be enough to entertain Candy.

Candy plopped onto the bed with her, forcing Hazel to pull her covers up to her chin to compensate for the drop-in temperature.

"Well, it's better than nothing."

CHAPTER FIVE
The Girl in the Window

Hazel and Candy headed out the door and to the elevator so Candy could show her around her new neighborhood. Although Hazel preferred to not leave the house at all, Candy wouldn't hear it. It seemed she would not be enjoying a quiet day at home after all. Most of her block held older homes and small apartment complexes, aside from the university and the hospital, which were the largest structures nearby. It was Candy who led the way, pointing out various hangouts and homes from her past. Thoughts of Candy's murder continued to find its way into Hazel's mind, but she fought back the urge to bring it up. She knew her new friend didn't want to talk about it, but she hoped that the conversation would happen one day.

Passing Loyola University's Marquette Hall, Hazel admired the gothic architecture that transported her back to the European Renaissance. It looked like a castle, ominous, with its dark brick, arches, and turrets. Although beautiful and interesting, something about the building gave her a feeling of trepidation, sending her heart into her stomach. Movement in a fifth-floor window caused her eyes to be drawn upward, only to see a pale face staring back at her. She stopped in her tracks. She stood there, on the corner of the street, staring up at the face, but it did not make any sudden movements. The woman, face gaunt and hair straggly, appeared to be wearing some sort of gown, possibly a hospital gown.

"Do you see her?" she asked Candy, who stopped her incessant chattering.

"Who are you asking about, doll?" Head turning from side to side, Candy looked for the mystery woman.

When Hazel raised her trembling hand to the window, she watched the emaciated woman retreat, leaving nothing behind but darkness.

"I don't see anyone, doll. Was she up there?" Candy pointed towards the building, squinting.

With a slow nod, Hazel confirmed Candy's question, shrugging her shoulders as she turned to walk again.

"She's gone. She looked sick or something. Do you have any idea what a hospital patient would be doing up there?"

"No, sorry, doll. I'm not sure. That's creepy though."

"Yeah, she was. Hey, I'm kind of ready to head home. It looks like it's going to storm."

Candy looked up at the sky, undeterred. Rain didn't bother her, so she didn't seem conscious of the weather.

"Okay," she muttered, clearly disappointed.

They hadn't quite made it back to the apartment when the first sprinkles of rain came down. Hazel pulled her jacket over her head to keep dry. Goodness knows she had no intention of washing her hair if it got drenched and tangled.

Getting back into the apartment, she threw off her wet clothes and changed into a pair of fluffy pajamas. After changing, she put on a pot of coffee and proceeded to unpack the boxes that she and Tate had brought in the day before. He had helped to unpack a few before he left to go to work, but she still had plenty more to go through. At first, Candy tried to play supervisor, telling Hazel where she had kept her own belongings, but Hazel eventually shooed her away, so Candy ended up on the sofa watching murder mysteries while Hazel worked in peace.

Once she emptied a handful of boxes, she made her way over to sit next to Candy on the sofa, pulling out her laptop so she could research Marquette Hall at Loyola University.

The first thing she noticed was that the building was built in 1910, which gave her over one hundred years of spirits to search through. She knew that a structure of such an age would be crawling with resident ghosts. It didn't take her much more reading to find something that made her gasp, made the hair on the back of her neck stand up. According to the history, in the first five years of its existence, the hospital had used the fourth and fifth floor of Marquette Hall for anatomy courses, meaning that students would go to those floors to take classes in which they would dissect cadavers. She also read about how the building didn't initially have elevator access to the fifth floor, so they rigged a crane to lift the bodies up into a stairwell which the students used as well.

Bile rose in her throat as the morbid details soaked into her mind. The spirit in the window wasn't there because she died there, in a hospital. She was most likely there because they had studied her body there, dissected her in the name of science. With so many bodies used for this purpose, Hazel felt it impossible to discover who this woman could be or why she was hanging around. Impossible, unless she went there to speak to her, although she didn't know if that would pan out either. However unlikely it may have been, she felt it her duty to at least try to cross the spirit over. It was in a spirit's best interest to cross the veil and not remain in an old school, where she probably had no reason to be, with no history to keep her there. Closing her laptop, she attempted to close her mind as well from the visions of what the spirits in Marquette Hall had experienced as they watched their earthly bodies carved up. Instead, she turned to Candy with a proposition.

"I have an idea for tomorrow," she said, disturbing Candy's television show.

Candy looked up at her, her blue eyes wide. "What are you thinking, sugar?"

"Well... I'll invite Tate over tomorrow so you can gawk at him... if you come with me to the fifth floor in Marquette Hall over at Loyola University."

Her eyebrows furrowing, it was clear Candy was confused.

"That doesn't sound like a fair trade. What would you want to go there for?"

"Honestly, I want to speak with the spirit I saw today, if I can. She looked like she was in awful shape. I'd like to see if I can help her."

"Oh," Candy trailed off. "Sounds spooky. I'm in."

"Good! Well, I'm off to bed. Stay out of trouble, will you?"

With a smirk, Candy waved her hand in the air. "What kind of fun would that be?"

Chapter Six
The Marquette Hall Morgue

Hazel woke up from a fitful night of sleep, but she didn't remember any of her dreams. With all the nightmares that plagued her in her sleep, she didn't doubt that she was forgetting some, but felt glad for the amnesia. The day was already going to be a challenge, even without her reeling from a traumatizing night of sleep.

Trudging into the living room, she saw Candy, bright-eyed and bushy-tailed, which was a state that Hazel would never be caught in so early in the morning. She did a double take when she noticed Candy was wearing a different outfit than she had been the night before. Scratching her head in confusion, she made her way to the kitchen to turn on the coffee pot.

"Um, Candy... How are you wearing different clothes than yesterday?"

Candy giggled. "I learned how to change my outfit shortly after I died. There was no way I was going to spend the rest of my afterlife in a blood-stained work uniform."

"Hmm." Shrugging, Hazel turned around to pour a cup of coffee. "Okay, then. I'll ask no more. You look great."

"Well, of course I do, love."

Candy stood up to twirl. She was wearing a spaghetti-strap green dress that made her fiery red hair stand out even more. In addition to her perfectly red lips, her excessively long locks were curled into a stylish hairstyle that would have been the stuff of a glamor photo shoot.

"You know Tate can't see you." Although it was only a joke, Hazel realized it may not have been funny. As it turned out, Candy had a sense of humor, so she laughed, rather than getting upset.

"I know that, silly. But I still needed to look better than you."

Hazel's mouth dropped at the insult, but Candy simply stuck out her tongue like a mature adult. Their middle school banter made Hazel smile. After spending so much time in law school, it was quite a welcome change.

"Anyway… are you ready to go?"

"Yep!"

As they retraced their steps back to Loyola University, Hazel felt anxiety creep over her. Marquette Hall's history freaked her out, and she was unsure of what she would find on the fifth floor. There was no guarantee she would be able to get inside the building. Although she hoped for minimal security at the door, she didn't know what to expect. Stopping just outside of the building, she reached within herself to build up her protective walls. No matter what she found inside, she didn't want to go in mentally unprepared.

"Well, the spirits won't come to you, so are you ready to go inside?" Candy asked, a slight snark in her tone.

"I suppose." Hazel sighed, although she wasn't truly ready.

Getting into the building was easier than she had expected. There didn't seem to be a lot of activity outside of the building, so she assumed the students were in class. The building had no one guarding the entrance. She thought it best to take the stairs instead of the elevator but regretted that decision by the time they had reached the third floor. Although she was quite thin, she didn't work out. Panting as though she had run a marathon, she opened the door to the fifth floor and felt immediately assaulted by a drop in the temperature. Although there were no dead bodies on the floor, it was certainly cold enough to do so. Judging from the temperature of the other floors, Hazel did not believe it to be the air conditioner causing the change in temperature, so she warily glanced around, looking for any lingering spirits.

Stepping into the main hall, they tried to map out where the spirit of the young woman had been the day before. It was eerily quiet. If classes had been going on, she couldn't hear them from outside in the hallway. Taking a right, she found her way to the end of the hall and then quietly listened outside the door where she believed the spirit to be. Not hearing any sounds from within, she slowly opened the door and squeezed inside.

Thankfully, the room looked to be used for storage, so if she was quiet, she didn't expect anyone to walk in and catch her in there. Browsing the contents of the room, she discovered that many of the boxes held old patient files and belongings, including things she expected should have been returned to the families of the deceased. Some files were so old, however, that it surprised her the school still had them.

"Is there anyone in here with me?" she whispered. "I can see you, and maybe help you, so please show yourself."

Sensing no change in the atmosphere, she continued to look through the room, which was quite large, hoping the female spirit would show herself. She didn't want her break-in to the school to have been for nothing.

"Do you see anyone?" she asked Candy, but Candy shook her head, continuing the scan on the opposite side of the room.

Making her way to the window, Hazel shuffled around boxes to look outside, realizing it would have been difficult for any living person to look through that window the day before. It took more effort for her to get a view out of it than she expected, because there were several boxes stacked just in front of it. After doing a bit of climbing, she could peer outside to the grounds below. Everything was quiet. There was a bit of traffic on the street, which was the usual in downtown New Orleans, but the school grounds had appeared sparsely populated. She almost wondered if it was a holiday she didn't know about.

Stepping back from the window before someone could see her through it, she did a double take as she noticed another reflection staring back at her. A young woman, possibly in her teens, wearing a white hospital gown, looked back at her from the reflection in the window. Her face was so thin that it was almost skeletal. Feeling the hair on the back of her neck stand up, Hazel stared at the girl for a long moment, unsure how to proceed. She didn't want to scare the spirit away, but she felt concerned that any sudden movement would do just that.

"Find anyone yet?" Candy called out from behind the boxes, causing Hazel to jump. Thankfully, the spirit did not stir, and instead stared blankly back at her.

"Shh... She's here."

Taking a chance and hoping she wouldn't scare the spirit away, Hazel slowly turned around to face her, putting her back to the window so she could look into the face of the woman, and not just the reflection. She looked remarkably solid, as though Hazel could reach out and touch her, but she did not dare to try. Hazel pushed back the shivers she felt from being in such close contact with the spirit and turned up the corners of her mouth in a weak smile.

"My name is Hazel. What's yours?"

The girl looked at Hazel with a confused look on her face, head tilted as though she were trying to understand Hazel's words. Maybe she was trying to understand how Hazel could see her, but Hazel wasn't sure.

"What's your name?"

Straightening her tilted face, the spirit's eyes opened wider, seeming to realize Hazel could see her. When she reached out to touch Hazel, almost as though to make sure she was real, Hazel braced herself against the coolness of her touch. A chill ran down Hazel's spine when the girl touched her face. After quickly withdrawing her hand, the spirit twisted her fingers into one another before pulling them up against her belly. As Hazel glanced over the young woman's shoulder, she saw Candy's crimson mane in the background, her nervous gaze shaking Hazel's confidence.

"You can see me?" The tone of her voice was small and timid. As her ghostly form flickered, the girl hesitated. "How?"

Her eyes were fixed on Hazel in astonishment, like Hazel was a mythical creature she had only ever heard about in stories.

"Yes," Hazel kept her voice low and steady. "I can see you. I'm not sure how. I've always been able to see people like you. Why are you still in this place?"

Looking around, the girl raised her hands at her sides. Her eyes scanned the area around her, as if she were trying to recall where she had been and how she had gotten there. Hazel could see emotion wash over the girl's face as the realization hit her that she didn't know where she was.

"I don't know." The spirit's face crumpled under the weight of a sob. "Where am I?"

Hazel didn't know how to answer the question. She didn't want to tell the girl that she was in a building where her body had been cut open and studied like a frog in a biology class. Her stomach dropped just thinking about it. The girl looked at her with an intense stare, waiting for a response Hazel didn't know how to give, so she changed the subject instead.

"What is your name? Maybe I can find out where you should be."

Before the young woman could answer, the doorknob creaked as the door opened. She ducked quickly behind the boxes, and the girl vanished. Hazel could hear two men speaking in the doorway, so she got as low as she could, hoping they would leave quickly and not discover her there. She heard a shuffling of boxes, then a box being dropped on the floor, before the door slammed shut again. Chancing a peek over the side of the boxes that were giving her cover, she saw she was alone in the room again. The men had left, and so had the spirit. Just as she lowered herself back behind the boxes, trying to slow her breathing, Candy floated over next to her, sitting casually on the top of the stack.

"They're gone," said Candy. "Are you ready to get out of here?"

"When the coast is clear. I don't think she's going to come back today." Hazel huffed out a breath, disappointment squeezing her chest.

"Okay. I'll go look."

Rising from the stack of boxes, Candy floated through the door to check the hall.

Chapter Seven

Unwanted Memories

Hazel texted Tate on their way back to the apartment to see if he wanted to get together and watch a movie. She wanted to see him, but she also had to keep her end of the deal with Candy, so she was grateful when he accepted. No sooner did she get home and change clothes than he was knocking on her door with a smile on his face and a pizza in his hands. He never failed to make her crush on him grow, although she'd never tell him that.

With the pizza box between them, they sat on the sofa and flipped through the options until they found a thriller to watch. In the chair across from them, Candy stared at Tate as if he was fresh meat, making Hazel regret their arrangement. She was grateful, at least, that Tate couldn't see Candy, because she was drilling a hole with her eyes right through his chest. Despite her best efforts,

Hazel was unable to concentrate on anything else. Despite her repeated attempts to push Candy away, she seemed to be taking their deal seriously, gawking at him until he left. Despite this, she felt bad for Candy. She couldn't imagine being in Candy's position, no longer having the ability to be close to a man, even though Hazel didn't use that freedom to the best of her abilities. One day, if she ever got the nerve, she would need to change that.

Saying goodbye to Tate that night was hard. Each night he left without her telling him how she felt made her feel like she was one step closer to losing him to someone else. He was a great catch, so it was only a matter of time before he settled down with a woman who wasn't her. Their friendship had always been flirty, but she never thought his flirtation was anything more than a joke. Even though he always came running to her beck and call, she didn't expect him to be genuinely interested in her. He was a great friend, and she couldn't imagine him wanting anything more. No matter how much she liked him, however, she didn't feel good enough for him, which was sad, but it was the way it was.

Heading to bed that night, thoughts ran through her mind at a dizzying speed. She would start a new career at the public defender's office in only a few short days, so if she was going to help the young spirit in the university, she needed to do it soon. But she had a fresh fear of going back to the university. She had come so close to getting caught, which made her even more uneasy about trying her luck again, although she didn't feel like she had much of a choice. Helping spirits cross over was her obligation, so she couldn't turn her back on the girl, no matter how uncomfortable returning to the university made her feel.

Sitting on the floor in the corner of the room, I watched as he held onto me, holding pressure over the wounds on my back as the life poured out of me like paint onto the carpet. I knew I was gone, but he still tried diligently to save me. My heart longed to be back there, in my body, so I could tell him thank you, thank you for trying so hard to save me. But it was no use. I couldn't do anything except sit in the room's corner, watching in a blind panic, as the power of my being was stripped from me. The tears welled up in my eyes, dropping onto my hands in a steady stream. I thought for a moment they looked like little diamonds because of how the reflection of the light added a hint of a sparkle to them.

My attention turned back to him as he continued trying to put breath back into my lungs, as he tried to make my heart beat once again. But I knew that nothing he could do was going to bring me back. My new form felt surprisingly numb, and I hated it. I wanted to feel the good and the bad. I wanted to be alive. I crawled to him, trying to tell him it was okay to let me go, but before I could touch him, he realized the truth for himself. The others moved around him in a frenzy. I knew they were there, but I couldn't stop watching him, the man who gave saving me all that he could. I watched him lean back to sit on his heels, as another man draped a white sheet over me, and then patted him on the shoulder, as if to tell him he had given it his best. Unable to look at myself in that way for another second, I wiped a tear from my cheek, gave him a kiss on his, and walked into my bedroom. I knew he would never know how much I appreciated him, but I would never forget.

Hazel woke up from another nightmare, but this one had taken her breath away. Sitting up in bed, she gasped for air, allowing her tears to burst through. Her dream was a scene she had never wanted to witness. It only took her a moment to realize that she had witnessed the moment when Candy's spirit had separated from her body. She watched as Tate had tried desperately to save a woman he didn't even know. Being a police officer, he always got called to scenes, but she never realized it was Tate who had been called to Candy's apartment when she was stabbed to death. Neither he nor Candy had even seemed to realize the connection that they had. Candy did not seem to recognize him, and he never mentioned having been in her apartment before. Maybe he realized, but he didn't want to tell Hazel and freak her out, knowing that a woman had been murdered in her new place. Maybe Candy recognized him, but she had insisted that she didn't want to discuss her murder, so Hazel had no way to know for sure. Whatever the case, she only wished she could block what she had seen in her nightmare out of her memory. Instead, she knew it would probably haunt her forever.

Before she could give it any more thought, and before Candy could come in and start asking questions, Hazel got out of bed and jumped into the shower. She didn't want to bring up the contents of her nightmare with Candy and cause Candy to have to relive that night all over again. She was determined to erase it from her mind in any way she could, including with soap and water.

"Good morning!" With a bright smile, Candy's head popped through the shower curtain as though it wasn't even there.

Hazel, too stunned to react, stood there, naked and drenched, for a few awkward moments.

"Uh... good morning. Why is your head in my shower?"

"I missed you!"

"I miss you too, but can you give me about five minutes to finish up here?"

"Oh, yeah, for sure."

To Hazel's relief, Candy backed out of the shower and left the bathroom.

Once she knew Candy was gone, Hazel finished showering and got ready for the day. She was already feeling on edge after the nightmare she had suffered, so getting ready to return to the haunted university did not help her state of mind one bit.

Heading into the kitchen, she found Candy at the coffee pot, trying to turn it on. As Hazel approached, Candy seemed to redouble her efforts. "I was trying to get this going for you, love. A little more practice and I think I'll be able to do it perfectly."

"I appreciate the effort." Moving beside her friend, Hazel took over the task "You're actually able to do a lot more than I expected you to be able to do, especially since you've only been in this state for about a year. How did you learn to do so much stuff in such a short time?"

"Boredom and practice, love. I have had little to do over the past year except chase away potential renters." Candy shrugged her shoulders as though scaring away living people was a necessary part of her job. Hazel shot her a side eye, before allowing a grin to take its place.

"Well... I'm glad you chased them all away, so the apartment would be available for me."

"Me too." With a flirty grin, Candy blew Hazel a kiss.

CHAPTER EIGHT
The Wedding Ring

The weather was steamier on their second trip into the university, so much so that Hazel had pulled off her sweater and tied it around her waist. Sweaters weren't a usual fashion choice during the early summer in south Louisiana, but she remembered how cold the fifth floor had been before and wanted to be prepared. Just as the day before, there was no security guarding the doors to Marquette Hall, which allowed her to walk into the building unchecked. Also, like the day before, the halls were quiet, minus a few straggling students and staff who hurried along, trying to get to their destination. None of them even gave her a second glance, as she walked through the large foyer and into the stairwell.

"Just walk in like you own the place," Candy instructed her, although she didn't have the bravado to do so. She scurried more than strode.

Trudging up five flights of stairs was no easier the second time around, causing her to stop and pant multiple times along the way.

"You really should work out."

Hazel pulled herself a step higher, rolling her eyes. "Easy for you to say, Casper."

As though her life depended on it, Hazel held onto the railing, pulling herself upward.

Preparing for the frigid temperatures awaiting her on the other side of the door, Hazel stopped and put on her sweater before opening it. Not seeing anyone in the immediate area, she allowed the door to shut behind her. She tiptoed towards the right, reentering the same room where she had found the spirit of a woman the day before.

When Hazel entered the storage room, the spirit was already there, as though she knew Hazel was coming. A warm smile crawled across Hazel's face as she approached the timid spirit, motioning to Candy to give them privacy. This time, the girl seemed less afraid of her, smiling back at her.

"I thought you might return," the girl said in a soft voice, reaching out to touch Hazel's face again. The coolness of the touch sent a shiver through her body.

"Yes... I came back to help you. I'm sorry about yesterday. I think you were about to tell me your name. Do you remember your name?"

The girl thought for a moment as she glanced down at her hands, examining them as though they held the key to her identity. "I think my name is Mary."

"Do you know anything else? Your last name maybe? Or when you died?"

There was a distressed look on the girl's face, her eyes glassy and wide.

"I... I don't know," she stammered. "I keep being drawn here. That is all I know for sure."

As she reached out to touch Mary's arm, Hazel nodded.

"It's okay. We will figure this out. Maybe you're being drawn to something in these boxes."

Examining the girl closer, Hazel tried to at least narrow down the decade in which she may have lived. It was hard to tell with her wearing only a hospital gown, but her hairstyle was distinct. She thought the hairstyle may have been popular in the fifties or sixties, so she started looking through the boxes for one from that time period. The stacks against the window were some of the oldest, with some even dating back to the twenties, so she did her best to move the topmost boxes quietly, so she could get inside the box dated nineteen-fifty through nineteen-fifty-five.

The box was large and filled to the top with brown files that had barely legible names scrawled across them. She looked over the boxes, glancing around for Candy's spectral form that should have been somewhere in the room, but the clutter made it impossible to see.

"Candy," Hazel whispered. "Can you give me a hand?"

With a low popping sound, as though she had opened a jar that still had its seal, Candy manifested right beside her, causing her to jump.

"Ready and willing!" Although Candy exclaimed with more pep than Hazel felt was warranted, she appreciated it.

Opening another box and setting it beside the one she was searching in, she asked Candy to look through one while she looked through the other. She wanted to find any files for a woman named Mary. It was all the information she had to go on.

After about forty-five minutes of searching, she was dusty and starving, but undeterred. She was insistent on finding Mary's file before leaving, because she did not want to return to the university ever again. Giving up on the boxes for the nineteen-fifties and the nineteen-sixties, she dug through one decade earlier, the nineteen-forties. She couldn't imagine Mary having lived in the nineteen-seventies, not with her ski slope hairdo.

She had only gotten about a fourth of the way down into the box before she found a file for a seventeen-year-old girl named Mary Foret. The file was old and frayed on the edges, so she opened it delicately, careful not to tear the already tattered pages. The first page appeared to list general information, including Mary's name, date of birth, and other identifying facts. Hazel flipped ahead, revealing the second page, which was a photograph of Mary's remains laying on top of an autopsy table. She closed the folder quickly, hoping Mary had not seen the picture of her body. Glancing over her shoulder, she realized Mary had seen it. Tears fell from the young woman's eyes as she looked down at the folder in horror. Hazel's face fell as guilt swam over her. She dropped the folder to the ground like it had bitten her, eyeing it in disgust.

"Please... please keep going. It's okay. I know what I am."

Hazel reluctantly picked the folder back up, being careful to skip the second page, avoiding a second look at the gruesome photo. The third page appeared to be a death certificate, with notes stating what was found in the autopsy.

"Tuberculosis." Hazel looked back at Mary for confirmation. "You died from tuberculosis."

A grim expression appeared on Mary's face when she closed her eyes in thought for several beats before nodding.

As Hazel looked back down at the folder, a small, folded piece of cloth fell out of it, landing on the floor next to her foot. She looked down at it in surprise. Squatting down to pick it up, she slowly unwrapped the cloth, until a hint of gold flashed within the folds. Pulling out the small object and examining it in her hand, she realized it was a wedding band. She glanced back at Mary with the ring in her palm, hoping it would jog the young girl's memory. Maybe the ring had kept Mary in the university. As Mary's eyes locked onto the ring, something within her shifted. She reached for it, manipulating it only slightly without a corporeal form.

"That was my mother's." Mary sighed and wiped a tear from her eye. "It shouldn't be in a box in this dusty, old room."

Fighting back her own onset of emotions, all Hazel could do was nod.

"Where would you like it to go? Maybe I can take it there for you."

Mary's eyes lit up, relief spreading over her face.

"With her... It should be with my mother."

"Okay. I'll try to find her."

Returning her attention to the pages within the file, she came across a birth certificate that listed Mary's mother and father. Taking a picture of the document with her cell phone, she put the ring into her pocket, and then placed the file back into the box, along with the rest of the paperwork she had pulled out.

"Do you know how to find her?" she asked, and Mary quickly nodded. "Okay. Then let's return this to her."

CHAPTER NINE
Moving On

This time, when Hazel and Candy left Loyola University's Marquette Hall, Mary was at their side. She had a renewed sense of purpose, and that was to return her mother's wedding ring to where her mother was laid to rest. Thankfully, Mary's mother was buried in one of the largest cemeteries in New Orleans, so they didn't have far to go. The sun was getting low on the horizon, but Hazel intended to return the ring before heading home. She didn't want Mary to have to wait one day longer for the rest she desperately deserved.

Walking into the St. Louis Cemetery, a rekindled sense of dread washed over Hazel. Not because she was in a place where the dead were at her feet, but because the cemetery had fallen into a state of disrepair. Although it was a very old cemetery that had been neglected for a long time, Hurricane Katrina had caused devastating damage to it, leaving tombs broken and human remains exposed. Since most of New Orleans was below sea level, most of the tombs stood above the ground, like ominous reminders of the finiteness of life. It did not hold the same energy as a cemetery with neat crosses and headstones sticking out of the ground. Hazel fought her own uneasiness and kept putting one foot in front of the other, following Mary's spectral form that glided with a purpose.

Mary stopped just in front of a large weather-beaten mausoleum. Hazel could tell that it had once been white, but it had now become brown, and grass grew out from its roof. It was almost ironic how life fought to survive in this space meant for the dead. The crypt had the name 'Foret' engraved on the front in large letters.

"This is it," Mary said, pointing to the front of the monument. "She is inside."

Swallowing back an enormous lump of fear, Hazel nodded her head once and stepped forward to the door of the crypt. The lock was broken but the door's hinges were rusted, causing the door to refuse to open. Looking around, she found a piece of wrought-iron fence and used it to wedge the door open, causing a high-pitched squeal as it revealed its contents to her. She choked on the scent of dank earth and rot that escaped through the opening. The scent was so pungent that it coated her tongue. Turning on her phone's flashlight, she took one more hesitant glance at Mary and Candy before squeezing herself through the opening.

There were shelves on either side of her, stacked up like prison bunk beds, but the darkness was so thick that her flashlight hardly made a difference. Mary had come in behind her, helping to illuminate the darkness with her spectral form. Hazel had to pull her collar over her nose and mouth just to protect her lungs from the assault of the disgustingly thick air. She looked to her left to see that Mary had dropped to her knees beside one of the shelves in the tomb.

"Is this her?" Hazel closed the distance between them, trying her best to watch her step in the darkness.

Wiping a tear from her eye, Mary nodded her head slowly, gently passing her hand over the figure that was hidden beneath the cloth. Reaching into her pocket, Hazel pulled out the gold ring and set it softly on the chest of Mary's mother. Mary looked up at her with a sad smile before looking back down at her mother.

"She's waiting for you, you know. All you have to do is cross and you will find her."

Although Mary did not respond, Hazel knew she understood.

She quickly climbed back out of the tomb, but she watched as Mary looked back at her, smiling sweetly, before being enveloped in light, and a wave of warmth passed over Hazel's body. She felt an enormous sense of relief.

After Mary crossed over, she and Candy walked out of the cemetery together. It was getting dark, and Hazel didn't want to be caught in the cemetery at night. Not only was it against the rules, but it wasn't a safe place to be.

"So, is this what I have to expect while I'm hanging out with you?" A smirk spread across Candy's full lips.

"Yup."

"Well, alright. Sounds like fun," Candy grumbled, before looking at Hazel with a gleaming smile, making her friend laugh.

"Good! Now let's go home."

Candy's Story

CHAPTER TEN

New Love

C andy Townsend watched the clock behind the bar change to 1:40 A.M. Only twenty more minutes before she could shoo the raucous crowd onto the street and head home. She had plans after work and was looking forward to them. Her estranged boyfriend, Brad, was at work, so she didn't have to worry about him showing up at her door. Trying to break it off, saying the words repeatedly, didn't seem to have much effect. He kept pretending he hadn't heard them. She hoped he would eventually find someone else, like she had. She was moving on. She was in love.

She had met Jake through Brad, sort of. Jake had known Brad since they were in high school, however Brad's narcissistic personality had caused a wedge in their relationship just as it had between him and Candy. Jake was twenty-six, three years older than her, but she appreciated the age difference. He was mature. He had his life together. He wasn't a boy playing in a man's world. Plus, his dark hair and dark eyes were irresistible to her.

Candy, with her large blue eyes, thigh-length crimson hair, and extroverted personality, got a lot of attention in the bar industry. None of those men interested her, though. She only had eyes for Jake. Sure, she had to pretend to flirt when at work. It was how she paid her bills as a bartender in the city of New Orleans, but most of it was just an act. She loved men, but contrary to popular belief, she was capable of monogamy.

"Come on!" begged Hera. Hera was Candy's best friend, colleague, and New Orleans' number one gay bar aficionado. "Let's go to Lavender Line!"

Hera ran her fingers through her pastel hair, throwing a seductive wink at a young blond woman who had walked into the bar. Flirting was her default setting, and she was damn good at it.

"You are bad... and you may be the lesbian version of me, but I can't go tonight. I'm seeing Jake."

Hera frowned but Candy watched as a new idea developed in Hera's head. Her frown turned upside down to reveal an impish grin.

"He can come! I've barely gotten to know him. He's so quiet. Maybe I just need to get him drunk…"

"Ha. He's more on the shy side, so I don't think getting him drunk will make much of a difference. I don't mind his introversion though. I don't think a relationship could handle two people like me."

Candy batted her big blue eyes innocently, making Hera smirk.

"You'd never sleep. That's for sure."

Candy grinned.

"Oh, don't you worry. We still don't sleep much. He may be quiet, but he is delicious."

Gasping and acting surprised, Hera swatted Candy on the arm.

"You dirty dog! So, will you come with me to Lavender Line? Pretty please! Bring Jake along. I need a new woman in my life, and I won't find one here."

Candy laughed loudly and several patrons turned to stare at her.

"That's a laugh! You need to get rid of a few! How many do you have currently? Like six?"

Grunting loudly and flipping her hair in her hand, Hera turned dramatically on her heel and began cleaning the bar. Candy wasn't even sure how she kept all her girlfriends straight in her head. She was like the female version of Glenn Quagmire. Candy wasn't complaining, though. She was impressed. She gave Hera one more sideways glance before pulling out her cell phone to send a text message to Jake. She quickly asked if he'd like to go to Lavender Line with Hera, then began her own end-of-night procedures. The bar would not clean itself, and someone needed to raise the broom and clear the customers out of the building by pretending to swat them. It may have been unconventional, but it worked.

After closing the bar, the dynamic duo made their way to Lavender Line to meet Jake and the future Mrs. Hera Blanchard. Candy touched up her makeup in the rearview mirror while Hera drank from a half-empty bottle of tequila. They had parked a few blocks away from Lavender Line, but Jake agreed to meet them at a shop nearby. Getting out of Hera's hatchback, which was parked hastily along the street, a familiar set of dark eyes caught Candy's attention.

"Hey!" she squealed as she jumped out of the car and wrapped her arms around Jake, who was leaning against a streetlamp.

"Hey, to you. You look beautiful."

She planted a deep kiss on his lips before twirling in place.

"Thank you, muffin! So, do you!"

"Hey, good lookin," Hera said as she approached the lovers. Jake blushed.

"Hey, yourself."

Hera wrapped Jake in a ferocious hug, nearly toppling him onto the street. When she pulled out of the awkward embrace, she wrapped her arm around his shoulders, steadying both. Hera had swallowed a few too many shots, and it showed. She patted Jake on the chest.

"Wow. You're a sturdy one. I bet Candy can literally climb you like a tree."

"Hera!" Swatting Hera's arm off her man, Candy dropped her face into her hands, muffling her laughter. Hera was undeterred.

"So." Hera bounced up and down with excitement. "Where to?"

"You're the one leading this charade. We're following you."

Locking elbows with Hera, and taking Jake by the hand, the group of three walked deeper into the French Quarter like a bright-haired and scantily dressed scene from the Wizard of Oz.

Candy woke up the morning after the gay club crawl with a massive headache. They had danced the night away, and she may have even sung some karaoke, but she couldn't remember all the details.

She briefly remembered Jake dropping Hera off at her house before driving back to her own apartment. She hoped Hera's car had survived the night unsupervised. Leaving your vehicle on the side of the street in the French Quarter overnight wasn't the wisest decision, but she was glad Hera hadn't driven home.

She glanced to the left to see Jake was still lying next to her, which did not happen often enough. With Brad still not accepting their breakup, she didn't want to cause a fight between the men by flaunting their relationship. It was complicated. It may have been silly to keep Jake a secret from Brad, but she was more so sparing Jake's well-being than sparing Brad's feelings. Things would settle down eventually.

She had not even invited Brad to her apartment in at least a month, which she expected to be a big enough hint that their relationship was over, but Brad was ignoring the signs. He was good at ignoring realities he didn't agree with.

Jake stirred before rolling over to face her. His dark eyes mesmerized her. He smiled warmly and his smile showed through his eyes. She traced her fingers down his chest, kissing him tenderly. She treated the moment like forbidden love, like she was hiding him away. She had to take in all of him she could, while the moment was upon her.

Cupping his face in her hands, she rubbed her thumbs through his beard.

"I love you; you know."

He wrapped his arms around her, surrounding her in his warmth.

"You do? I love you too."

Chapter Eleven
Slain

The bar was lively. Candy and Hera had little time to socialize with each other besides the yelling out of drink orders over the music. The patrons flooded into the bar like the Louisiana mosquitos. At least she'd make good tips. Her rent wasn't exactly cheap, but affordable or not, she was determined to live in the city. Downtown was where her job was, and it was where the people were. The people who kept her life from being as lonely as it could have been. She moved to the city specifically for city life, and she couldn't get that if she lived in a less expensive suburb.

It took them longer to leave the bar after closing that night. Many patrons had straggled, and the cleanup task was immense. She couldn't have been more ready when she stepped out of the door and onto the sidewalk. Candy watched the sky as she pulled on her jacket and headed home from work. It was a beautiful night. With fall creeping in, the night held a chill. She far preferred the chill in the air to the sauna-like summers. Zipping her jacket all the way to her neck, she headed south for the three-block walk to her apartment. The leaves crunched beneath her feet as she navigated the broken pavement, being careful not to fall on her face.

The building appeared deserted, not that she could expect anything different at two in the morning. It was eerily quiet. Traversing the empty lobby before hitting the three on the elevator, she readied her keys for the door.

Her cortisol rose as the elevator chimed, announcing she had arrived at the correct level. She wasn't sure where the nervousness had come from. She had arrived home in the middle of the night most nights of the week for two years. This time, however, she swore she felt eyes on her, but she didn't see anyone lingering in the hallway. She hurried to her door, only taking a few seconds to open it. Setting her keys and purse down on the kitchen table, she started to turn around and close the door, when she felt a sharp pain in her back.

It throbbed like a deadly spasm, causing her to drop to her knees. When she turned around to see if there was an intruder, all she saw was a vacant doorway. Puddles of blood circled around her, triggering her to panic. She clambered to the kitchen table, and the pain erupted all around her. Reaching up to the table, she grabbed her cell phone with trembling hands and dialed 911 before falling into unconsciousness.

She awoke sitting on the floor in the corner of the room. The transition from unconsciousness to consciousness felt disjointed and messy. It was like waking from a dream, but only barely. It took her several agonizing moments to gather her wits enough to survey her surroundings.

Her body lay in front of her, sprawled out across the kitchen floor, eyes staring, unblinking, at the ceiling. Candy examined the body she now peered out from. It looked the same, but it felt strange. Her new form felt surprisingly numb, and she hated it. She wanted to feel the good and the bad. She wanted to be alive. Her mind thought of Jake. Her family. The tears welled up in her eyes, dropping onto her hands in a steady stream. She thought for a moment they looked like little diamonds because of how the reflection of the light added a hint of sparkle to them.

A handsome police officer leaned over her. His face was tense with concentration. She watched as he held onto her, holding pressure over the wounds on her back as the life poured out of her like paint onto the carpet. She knew she was gone, but he still tried diligently to save her.

Her heart longed to be back there, in her body. She wanted to tell him thank you for trying so hard to save her. But it was no use. She couldn't do anything except sit in the room's corner, watching in a blind panic, as the power of her being was stripped from her. She wasn't in that body any longer, but she could still feel her life drain from it. She stared into her own unseeing eyes. It only hurt her more, but she couldn't help it. Maybe if she focused on them hard enough, life would return to them.

Her attention turned back to the officer as he continued trying to put breath back into her lungs, as he tried to make her heart beat once again. But she knew nothing he could do would bring her back.

Her heart ached. Not the physical one, but the philosophical one that lived in her consciousness.

The more he struggled to save her, the more desperate she felt. She couldn't take it. She crawled to him, trying to tell him it was okay to let her go, but before she could touch him, he realized the truth for himself.

The others moved around him in a frenzy. She knew they were there, but she couldn't stop watching him, the man who gave saving her all he could. She watched him lean back to sit on his heels, as another man draped a white sheet over her, and then patted him on the shoulder, as if to tell him he had given it his best.

Unable to look at herself in that way for another second, she wiped a tear from her cheek, gave him a kiss on his, and walked into her bedroom. She knew he would never know how much she appreciated him, but she would never forget.

Climbing onto her bed, she cried until the darkness consumed her. She didn't fight it. Anything was better than what she was going through at that moment.

Chapter Twelve
New State of Being

She didn't know how much time had passed when the front door jostled open. Candy hid in the closet, peeking through a crack in the door. A young woman, probably a college student, entered her apartment.

"Let me know if you have any questions," said a female voice from the corridor. Candy couldn't see who was standing out there, but she couldn't reveal her presence to check, not yet. She remained in her hiding spot, watching the girl quietly.

The girl seemed oblivious to her presence and instead, browsed the apartment methodically, even looking into Candy's refrigerator and cabinets. Candy could feel her annoyance grow as she watched helplessly. This was not okay. She wanted the unwelcomed stranger to leave, but she didn't know how to make that happen. She had to try something.

Throwing the closet door opened with more force than she thought possible, Candy rushed out of the closet and faced the intruder. However, in one unhampered motion, the girl stepped right through her, causing a temporary flourish in her belly.

What in the hell?

Candy gasped. She was taken aback. Why couldn't the girl see her? Her anger rose.

"Get out!"

As Candy screamed, the television turned on unexpectedly. The volume blared, catching the young girl's attention. They both stared at it in awe for several slow-motion moments. Then, the girl darted into the living room. Her eyes were wide with fear, but she didn't speak. Instead, the girl stared at the television as though it was a portal to hell and was paralyzing her to stay in that position. Positioning herself in front of the girl, Candy waved her hands wildly, trying to get the girl's attention, but to no avail.

The horrid memories flooded back. She was dead. Murdered. Of course, this girl couldn't see her. No one could. She was helpless and alone. Was this what she had to look forward to, an eternity stuck in the background, watching other people invade her space?

Summoning energy from somewhere, Candy grabbed the remote control and tossed it at the girl. It hit her stomach with a loud thump before it dropped to the floor. The following moments seemed to almost move in slow motion. The girl stared down at the fallen remote, not daring to touch it, before cradling her stomach in her hands and fleeing from the apartment, slamming the door in her wake.

No longer being alive, but still existing in the plane of the living, time moved in a nonlinear way. Candy no longer knew what day it was, or how much time had passed between her moments of consciousness. She could phase out her form when she was fatigued, although being fatigued in her spectral state felt different than it had when she was alive. People talk about seeing a bright light when you die, seeing the veil open for you to enter, but Candy shunned the light. She didn't know what was on the other side of that light, but she knew what was on her side. Her apartment was on her side, her security. Plus, she didn't completely mind her new state of being. Sure, she missed Jake, Hera, and her family, but she could still leave the apartment and people watch. She could move around as she pleased. There was a freedom to this new state she had never known before.

At first, she followed Jake, Hera, and even Brad, trying everything to get them to notice her. They never did. Eventually, being around them became too painful, so she stopped torturing herself and stuck to watching people she didn't have feelings for or attachments to.

She spent much of her time in her apartment. Her newfound powers of manipulating her environment were too intriguing to ignore, so she spent a lot of time honing those skills. She had not only learned how to turn on the television and change its channels, but also how to use short bursts of energy to touch and even throw items. She used that tactic repeatedly, anytime someone entered her apartment looking for a new place to live. The skill she was most proud of, however, was her ability to change her appearance. She was insistent on not spending her afterlife in a bloodstained bartender's uniform, so she learned how to concentrate her energy on whatever she wanted her appearance to be, and after some time, she developed the ability to change entire outfits, and even her hairstyle. Mastering this ability made her giddy, even if no one could appreciate it but her.

Chapter Thirteen

Kindred Spirits

A clicking of the apartment's doorknob caught Candy off-guard.

What is it going to take for this realtor to give it a break? No one is moving in here!

"Look around," a voice from the corridor said. "I'll wait here and make some phone calls. Let me know if you have questions."

Another intruder entered her apartment. The girl, probably in her mid-twenties, nodded at the realtor in acknowledgement and then turned to face the room. Her hair was a light brown, and she had hazel eyes that were magnified behind red-rimmed glasses. She didn't have on any makeup, but she was pretty, albeit mousy. She entered the apartment gingerly, peering around as though she were looking for someone, and not there to view the space. Candy dissolved her visible form and watched the young woman from the hallway. As though she felt a chill, the girl wrapped her arms around her chest, rubbing her arms to warm them. She moved with hesitation. She was nervous.

Flexing her newfound powers, Candy concentrated on the television being on, pleased with herself as the box boomed to life. Next, she reached for the remote control, tossing it to the floor. It may have been parlor tricks, but they usually worked to drive people out of her apartment. The intruder yelped, scanning the room once again, but she did not appear to be afraid. Instead, she looked more curious. Slowly, the girl walked over and turned off the television, but before she could walk away, Candy turned it back on. Instead of fleeing, she backed up and sat down on the sofa. Candy was flabbergasted, but she felt her energy waning. She wouldn't be able to throw anything else for a while. She sat across from the girl in the blue chair she had bought from a boutique around the block, but the girl continued to scan the room. As Candy expected, she didn't see her. Having relaxed her energy, Candy knew she was invisible.

"You're not scaring me," the girl whispered. "You might as well show yourself."

Candy eyed the girl warily.

Would she be able to see me if I manifested my energy?

Forcing her energy to surge, Candy manifested her visible form into the chair. The young woman's eyes widened behind her stylish glasses, but she remained quiet. Candy smirked, but sat still, allowing the girl to take her in. She hoped to be intimidating enough to make this new intruder flee the apartment like all the others, but the young woman only squared her shoulders and focused in on Candy.

"I can see you and I can hear you. What are you doing here?"

Candy rolled her eyes at the audacity of being asked why she was in her own apartment.

"This is my apartment, doll. So, what are *you* doing here?"

The young woman seemed to expect a different response than the one she received.

"You know that you're..."

"Dead? Yes, love. I know that. Regardless, this is still my place."

Candy waved her hand dismissively, turning to look away.

"What's your name?"

The young woman's words came out in a compassionate tone. It was clear she was trying to be sensitive.

"Candy. Now please let that realtor know my apartment is not for rent and go on your way."

Candy kept her face impassive, but the young woman was visibly struggling with Candy's attitude. The young woman steadied her voice.

"I'm sorry, Candy, but I can't do that. If it isn't me who moves in, it'll be someone else. If we could learn to live together, then you would at least have someone to talk to, unless you're willing to cross over, but they will not stop looking for a renter."

Candy rolled her eyes again. She didn't want to share her apartment with anyone.

"I'm not crossing over, or whatever you call it. I'm happy enough where I am."

Candy's voice got higher as her rant progressed. She was starting to feel desperate.

"I don't understand. Don't you want to see what lies beyond?"

The question hit Candy hard in the gut, but she did her best to act unphased. She didn't want this stranger to think she was an easy target, to think she would ever leave under pressure.

"No way, doll. There's still a party in this world and I don't intend to leave it just because some bastard stabbed me in the back."

The young woman flashed Candy a sympathetic smile, which only made her feel more annoyed. She didn't want sympathy. She wanted privacy.

"I'm really sorry that happened to you."

The realtor opened the door, peeking her head in, which caused both of them to jump. Candy scowled at her, although the realtor couldn't see her.

"Are you alright, Hazel? I'm still making phone calls but wanted to make sure you didn't need any help."

"No. I'm fine. I'm just trying to get a feel for the place."

"Oh, okay. I'll be right out here if you need me."

Hazel nodded quickly and stood up from the sofa, appearing to be looking around the apartment again. This time, however, Candy stood up and followed her, softening her attitude. This woman wasn't here to hurt her.

"So, do you really think they won't stop showing the apartment until they find a tenant?"

"You can't pay rent anymore, and they don't know you're still here. So yes, I believe that. It's me, or someone else."

Candy pondered Hazel's response for a moment, while pacing the room aimlessly. Hazel watched her, although she didn't interrupt Candy's thoughts.

If this is true, I could end up living with someone worse... maybe a stinky old man. Ugh.

Candy's decision was made for her. She would have no choice but to allow someone to live in the apartment. The least she could do was choose who.

"If you don't move in, I may end up with someone much worse. I guess I really don't have a choice, because I'm not going anywhere."

"Uh, thanks." Hazel hesitated. "I guess I understand why you don't want to cross over, but I still hope you'll give it some thought. There isn't much for you on this side of the veil, but I'm sure we can become great friends if not. I will support you either way."

Candy threw an arm over Hazel's shoulder and felt an instant connection. An electric buzzing flowed from Hazel's body and into Candy's arm. It was a sensation she had never felt before, but it drew her in. In some strange way, it made her feel alive, as though she belonged to the living world again.

She smiled at her new companion. She felt linked to this young woman somehow, and she intended to use her afterlife to find out why.

Haunted Holiday: The Soldier in the Stone Room

Chapter Fourteen
The Stone Room

"Where am I? What's happening?"

I tried to speak, but no words escaped my mouth. Faces loomed over me as I lay paralyzed on a hard surface. My memory was clouded and all hope of knowing how I'd gotten there was gone. Their conversations were just a warbled blend of words I didn't recognize. My eyes darted around the room, trying to draw recognition in someone or something. Stone walls. Dirt. Dead bugs littered the floor. I didn't know where I was, but I didn't think it was somewhere I would go willingly. It was filthy, and the air was stale, like no one had opened a window in a long time. But even with no windows, it was bone-chilling cold. My teeth chattered, but no one brought me a blanket. No one acknowledged me as I suffered.

"Where am I?"

Why could no one hear me? Were they ignoring me? I didn't know. My heartbeat thrashed between my ears as my pulse raced. Could they hear it too? Maybe they could hear it but didn't care.

Pain flooded my vision as I glanced down to see the blood saturating my pants. My mind focused on getting up and running, but my legs didn't move. My body couldn't move.

"Help me!"

CHAPTER FIFTEEN

New Traditions

"This has got to be the weirdest Christmas ever," Hazel said as she balanced precariously on a kitchen chair, trying to put the star on top of the Christmas tree. Her best friend and ghost extraordinaire, Candy Townsend, oversaw the process.

"It'll be the best Christmas ever because you have me! It's our first Christmas together." Candy stared at the tree, a dreamy look in her eyes. She'd attempted to use spectral energy to help Hazel decorate but was forced to give up after breaking three ornaments. She was better at throwing objects than delicately placing them in a specific place. "All I want for Christmas is that delicious hunk of man-candy that you call 'just a friend.'"

Turning away from the job at hand, Hazel forced a middle-school inspired eye roll in Candy's direction. Candy responded by sticking out her tongue. Their friendship consisted of moments like this, of them acting like teens instead of women aged twenty-three and twenty-eight. "You and I want the same thing, then."

A wide grin spread across Candy's face as she moved closer to Hazel, nearly making her fall. "But you could actually have him... I'm just saying." She held up her hands in mock defeat as she backed away.

Hazel shook her head before returning her eyes to the tree. She checked the star was secure before climbing off the chair and plugging in the string of lights.

"It needs more ornaments." Circling the tree, Candy evaluated Hazel's handiwork.

"Correction." Hazel folded her arms across her chest. "It has enough ornaments."

"Whatever you say," Candy said, as both women plopped onto the sofa. "What's your plan for today?"

Hazel leaned back and propped her feet on the coffee table. "I have no plans. I'm going to sit my ass right here and stare at this tree. After the nightmare I had last night, I need a little relaxation. Maybe I'll order a bit of food, since the refrigerator is empty."

"As usual."

"Hush, you. I'm the only person I have to worry about feeding and I don't require groceries."

"You need to become domesticated at some point, is all I'm saying. Tell me about the nightmare. Was it a spirit memory?"

Hazel shrugged her shoulders. "I'm honestly not sure. I don't recognize anything from it. The person looked like they were in a dungeon or something. The walls were stone, and the room was filthy. They were freaking out, bleeding and trying to get the attention of other people in the room, but no one seemed to acknowledge them. I don't even know if it's a man or a woman, for sure, but I think it was a man." Hazel rubbed her forehead, feeling a headache coming on. "One thing I'm a bit confused about was his clothing. It looked old, like not of this century old. If it was a spirit memory, I don't know how I would have run into him."

Candy stared at Hazel, leaning slightly closer. "Any idea what he wanted?"

"Help. He wanted help."

"Hm. That sounds depressing."

Rubbing her knees lightly, Hazel pulled her feet up under herself. "Yeah. It was."

"So, what now? Do you just wait for him to make contact?"

"It's all I really *can* do."

The chime of Hazel's cellphone interrupted their conversation. She dug into the sofa cushions to retrieve it. Candy leaned forward to see who had sent the text. The message was from Tate Cormier, Hazel's good friend from college.

"Ooh! Invite him over!"

Hazel shot Candy a sideways glance before unlocking the phone to read the message.

Tate had been Hazel's friend since their years in undergrad, which meant they'd been friends for the better part of a decade. Hazel had graduated with her undergraduate degree in political science before going to law school. She had finished law school only a few months before. Tate had earned his undergraduate degree in political science as well but opted to join the New Orleans Police Department after graduation. She had a growing crush on him ever since she had met him, although she was too shy to ever tell him. Her level of introversion was nearly debilitating. Just the idea of coming clean about her crush gave her anxiety. Plus, she didn't want to tell him about her ability to see and speak to the dead and risk him thinking she was insane, or worse, run the other way.

Her hereditary gift of being able to speak to and see the dead had passed down the maternal line of her family, although it was often more a burden than a gift. Spirits could be extremely pushy when they needed help, and her ability to hide from them was nonexistent. They could see her abilities no matter how much she looked at the ground and tried to ignore them. It's not that she had not tried, however. She often watched the ground when she walked, because making eye contact with them often ensured they would follow her to wherever she was going. They didn't follow the same rules as the living, so locked doors and walls were not a deterrent. Her feelings did not matter. She could not report them for stalking. If they wanted her help, they wouldn't give up until they got it. Because of that fact, spirits had often taken over her life, allowing her to think about nothing else until she solved whatever problem was keeping them from crossing over.

Obligations to the spirit world had torn apart her own parents' marriage until there was only a string holding them together. It had even created a rift in the relationship between Hazel and her father. Her experiences with her own family caused her to build up walls and rules for herself when it came to romantic relationships. As a rule, she stayed away from them, because she knew no man would be willing to put up with what she would put them through. It did offer her a bleak future, but it wasn't anything she felt she was able to fix.

There had been moments of temptation, however. Sometimes she wanted more than what a fling could give her, and even those were in short supply. And Tate was delicious. Candy was not exaggerating. He flirted with her often, although Hazel didn't take it seriously. She believed it to be a friendly flirt, not a romantic one, but it made her blush, regardless. His blue-gray eyes were dreamy. His dark hair was thick, and she wanted so badly to run her fingers through it. He was tall and muscular, and his hugs were always bear hugs. There wasn't one thing about him that turned her off, but she suffered in silence. He had no idea she wanted him, so they spent time together as "just friends," although she wished they could be so much more.

Once her phone was unlocked, Candy scooted right up next to her so she could read the message as well. She was an incredibly nosy best friend. Hazel shivered against the chill of having a spirit so close, but she clicked on her messaging app, opening Tate's message. It read "Hey! I'll be off work at 4 and wondered if you wanted to watch Christmas movies with me?"

She dared a glance at Candy, who wiggled her eyebrows comically.

"Stop doing that, you weirdo," she said, rolling her eyes.

"No way! Girl... He wants you. I'm telling you. You need to stop holding out on him. 'Watch Christmas movies with me' is code for Netflix and chill."

Hazel responded "Yes" to Tate's message before returning her gaze to Candy. "No, it doesn't. He probably just really likes Christmas movies and doesn't want to ask his police buddies."

Scrunching up her nose, Candy plucked through Hazel's hair. "You need to go get in that shower before he gets here. Your hair is greasy as day-old pizza. That is not sexy."

Hazel pulled her hair out of Candy's reach, attempting to swat her, but Candy simply vanished from the sofa and reappeared on the chair across the room. "My hair is fine."

"If you say so..."

Without another word, Hazel got up from the sofa and trudged into the bathroom, slamming the door behind her.

Climbing into the shower once the water was hot enough, she dreaded washing her hair. It was a commitment to wash her hair, since it would then require drying and brushing, and she wasn't feeling ready for a commitment. She chuckled at her own train of thought before dropping a dollop of shampoo into her hand and massaging it into her scalp.

Chapter Sixteen

A Ghost and a Movie

When Tate arrived after his shift, he had a brown bag in his hand and the smell of Chinese food drifted into Hazel's nostrils. Her mouth watered. As he always did when he saw her, he wrapped her in a scrumptious bear hug that melted her heart just a little.

"I hope you haven't eaten because I brought Chinese. I think I remembered what you like." He set the bag on the table before taking off his jacket and hanging it over the back of the chair. He had already changed out of his police uniform and was dressed in jeans and a navy-blue sweater that made his light eyes sparkle. Candy's voice broke her out of the moment.

"I think he knows exactly what you like," Candy said in a seductive voice that always sounded silly with her Cajun accent. With Tate looking at her, she did her best to ignore Candy's comment. The last thing she wanted was for him to see her talking to thin air.

"I haven't eaten, so I *am* starving, but you didn't have to do that. You're too good of a friend."

His smile grew as he grabbed two plates out of the cabinet. "I didn't have to, but I wanted to." Pulling the containers out of the bag, Tate set everything out in the middle of the table and pulled a chair out for her before taking his own.

"I'll be right back, but you can start eating." She glanced at Candy before heading to the bathroom, closing the door behind her. It only took a moment for Candy's mane of red hair to slide in through the wall.

"Did you want me to follow you in here?" Candy's huge blue eyes looked innocent, but they never fooled Hazel. She forced a scowl.

"Candy, I love you, but you need to vamoose. You're going to make me look crazy if you keep making comments like that. Don't you have something better to do than stare at us all night?"

Candy looked hurt but nodded slowly. "I have nothing better to do than stare at *him* all night, but I get your point, so I'll go entertain myself somewhere. Have fun, doll. I'll be back later." Before Candy had finished blowing Hazel a kiss, she faded from view. Taking a deep breath and blowing it out slowly, Hazel exited the bathroom and returned to the kitchen to join Tate at the table.

"Is everything okay?" he asked. He had yet to eat but had opened the containers and fixed his plate.

"Everything is great, and the food smells amazing." He smiled as she sat in her chair and shoveled a large serving of food onto her own plate.

After dinner, they sat down on the sofa and watched both Home Alone movies over an endless bowl of seasoned popcorn. Tate had brought his own seasoning blend from home, something he came up with himself that turned popcorn into magic.

"What's in this stuff?" Hazel asked over a mouthful of popcorn, nearly choking.

"It's a secret... If I tell you, then you won't have me over for movies anymore." He smirked at her as she tried to hide the blush on her face.

"I wouldn't be able to recreate it, anyway. My cooking abilities are nonexistent. I would burn plain popcorn, hence why I have none in my cabinets. It's a fire hazard."

He chuckled before pulling out his phone and texting her. The chime caught her by surprise.

"What are you texting me for?"

He grinned mischievously. "Now you have the recipe."

A flash of movement caught her eye, pulling her attention away from Tate and the movie. Uneasiness prickled her skin as she leaned forward, reluctantly trying to see what had moved into her room.

"I'll be right back."

She stood from the sofa and gingerly walked to the bedroom, shutting the door behind her. The hair on the back of her neck stood up as the temperature of the bedroom chilled her skin.

"Candy?" she whispered, scanning the room slowly for her best friend. Candy wasn't there, but a man stood in the room's corner. She wanted to scream but held back when she realized the man wasn't living. He was a spirit, and she didn't want to alert Tate of anything being out of the ordinary. She eyed the man warily as he stared back at her.

Pain was etched across his face. His eyes bulged against wet skin, slick from sweat. He looked to be about her age, late twenties, but she couldn't be sure with the mustache and long goatee that seemed out of place on his face.

He wore some sort of tattered uniform in a gray fabric. Two rows of gold buttons trailed down the breast of a long coat and a red and black belt wrapped around his waist. She had never seen anything like it. It looked old, not something men wear nowadays. He had a black cap, but it wasn't on his head. Instead, he held it against his chest with shaky hands.

Calming her own shaky hands at her sides, she walked a few feet closer to him.

"Who are you?" she whispered, trying to keep her voice low so Tate wouldn't hear her talking.

He glanced around the room reluctantly, ducking his head into a bow. "Private Miller, ma'am."

A quick knock on the bedroom door startled Hazel. She turned to look at the door and by the time she looked back in the man's direction, he was gone.

"Hazel," Tate called from the other side of the door. "Are you okay?"

With thoughts still racing in her head, trying to make sense of the spirit who had appeared in her bedroom, she darted to the door and slung it open.

"Yeah. I'm sorry about that. I had forgotten to take care of something earlier. I'm done now."

Tate's eyebrows drew together as he reached out to touch her shoulder. "Are you sure everything is okay?"

She smiled up at him, appreciating his concern. "Absolutely! Do you want to finish the movie?"

"Definitely."

They sat down on the sofa together as Tate pressed play on the paused television. She did her best to focus on the movie, and on Tate, but part of her mind remained on the spirit in her bedroom, hoping he didn't return.

CHAPTER SEVENTEEN

History of an Attack

I held my position and my gun as the Yankee ships closed in on us. Major General Mansfield Lovell had already retreated with most of my brothers, leaving only a handful of us behind to defend the fort, hoping the North would hit us on land instead. But Lovell was wrong. The Yankees weren't coming on land, and there was no doubt as their gunships filled the width of the muddy Mississippi River.

The firing lasted for several days. My head spun as blasts hit the fort, one after another. There was no rest, no break to treat the wounded or bury the dead. There was only chaos.

I wanted to jump off the wall, or in front of a mortar, just to make it stop. Maybe that was their plan.

Our leadership was absent. No one knew what to do anymore, so we did the only thing we knew how to do. Fought.

Hazel rubbed her eyes as she awoke from the strangest spirit-induced dream she had experienced in a while. She didn't know much about the man who appeared in her bedroom while she and Tate watched a movie, but she knew his name was Miller and that he was a private, a Confederate soldier. He spoke about the Mississippi River. She could see it clearly through his eyes in her dream. What she didn't know was why he was haunting her, or how he had gotten attached to her.

Opening her eyes, she scanned the room, looking for Candy. Although Candy left the apartment periodically to people watch in the city, she was usually inside of their apartment. She had been since Hazel met her.

Candy had been murdered in that apartment several months before Hazel moved in, refusing to leave and tormenting prospective tenants who stopped by to view the place. She met her match when Hazel entered the apartment, however, because Hazel could see her, and called her out for her tricks right away. Televisions turning on by themselves and remote controls flying across the room were not going to scare Hazel away.

Begrudgingly, Candy agreed to stop her antics and allow Hazel to move into her home. The realtor was not going to stop showing the place, so she didn't really have a choice. Hazel had been living there for several months and they had become fast friends. They depended on each other, giving each other the companionship they both needed, like sisters.

Not seeing Candy in the bedroom, Hazel rolled out of bed, wrapped a fleece blanket around her shoulders, and trudged into the living room. She stopped just as she entered through the doorway, staring at Candy as she lay on the sofa.

"I knew I'd find your couch potato butt out here. Whatcha watching?" Hazel made her way into the kitchen to turn on the coffee pot.

"The usual." The television shut off with a click before Candy appeared just atop the kitchen table. Her legs swung playfully like a pendulum.

"Ah, murder mysteries. Those aren't very Christmassy."

"But they were! It was a special about murders that took place on Christmas."

Hazel chuckled. "There's no way that's a thing." She stood as the coffee dripped, anxiously awaiting pouring the liquid into her mug, then into her mouth.

"I'm telling you. It's real. Do you want to watch?"

"I'll have to pass. I think I need to go to the library or something. I had another dream about that spirit. Shit! I didn't see you last night to tell you what happened!"

Candy began bouncing up and down, her eyes wide with anticipation. "Tell me! Did you finally have sex with Tate? I need details!"

Hazel forced out a cackling laugh that was only partially fake before setting her face into something sterner. "No. I did not have sex with Tate. That's not what I was trying to tell you."

Candy's smile fell into a dramatic pout. She drew a tear down her cheek with her finger. "Boo. What a bummer. Well then, what is it you wanted to tell me?"

Folding her arms across her chest, Hazel pursed her lips. "I don't know if I want to tell you. You're not going to like it."

"Well, now you have to tell me!"

"Our apartment is haunted."

Shooting Hazel a sideways glance before disappearing from the table and reappearing on the sofa, Candy sighed loudly. "Very funny."

Hazel followed her into the living room, sitting on the blue chair across from her. "I'm not making a joke about you. There was a guy in our apartment last night. In the bedroom. A dead guy."

Candy's eyes bulged. "That's not good. I hate when they show up in here. I wish there was a way to prevent that from happening. It's our home."

"I know. I agree."

"Was it the guy from the dreams?"

Hazel nodded. "I'm pretty sure it was. He appears to be a Civil War soldier. I don't know where in the world he found me, though."

Candy scratched at her chin, tilting her head until her abnormally long red locks grazed the floor. "Yeah... he's not your usual spook."

"You know I hate when you call them that."

"Yep. That's why I do it. So... the library, huh? Can I come?"

"I suppose, but only if you don't distract me. They close early today since it's Saturday, so I won't have a lot of time. You'll have to find a way to entertain yourself."

Hazel knew it was against her better judgement to take Candy anywhere. She was like a toddler who ran around and never stopped talking. The problem wasn't that other people could see her; it was that Hazel could not un-see her. Ignoring the energetically obnoxious redhead was nearly impossible. But, leaving her home every day while Hazel worked created enough of a guilty conscience, so she felt incapable of leaving her home when it wasn't work related.

"Scout's honor," Candy said, as she saluted. "I promise I'll behave."

Rolling her eyes, Hazel hopped off the sofa and went into her bedroom to get dressed.

Deciding to go to the main city library on Loyola Avenue, Hazel was a bit intimidated, but knew it offered her the best opportunity to find what she needed. She found a parking spot along the street and walked up to the large black and white building, admiring the eclectic collection of sculptures on the grounds. Candy floated alongside her, dressed to the nines as she always was, even though only Hazel could see her. Hazel, on the other hand, was dressed in her usual jeans and a sweatshirt. If she wasn't working, which required business attire, then she was dressed as casually as possible.

Approaching the circulation desk, she didn't even know exactly what she was looking for. She knew the spirit's last name and rank, as well as his approximate time period, but that didn't narrow it down by much. A guy, close to her age, with long dreadlocks and espresso skin, approached her. His smile widened as he greeted her.

"Hey, there. Need help finding anything?"

Hazel hesitated, still unsure how to phrase what she was looking for.

"Um, I think so... Although I'm not sure of the specifics. I'm looking for information on a Civil War soldier... I think Confederacy. His name was Private Miller, and he would have died during the war. That's all I know."

One eyebrow arched as he looked at her with a confused stare before quickly snapping himself out of it.

"Any idea where he was from? Was he from here?"

She felt her face grow hot. She wasn't fond of being put on the spot, even if she was making a request. She was the queen of introverts, which was why she struggled with her chosen career at the Public Defender's office.

"I'm not sure. Oh- I do know he was an active participant when the Union came down the Mississippi and attacked the fort, if that helps."

His eyebrows lifted slightly as he nodded. "That may help a lot. I have some documents in the archive room, if you'd like to look through those."

"Yeah. That would be great. Thank you."

"Absolutely. Follow me."

Opening the waist-high door of the circulation desk, he walked out from behind it and led her up the stairs to the City Archives and Special Collections room. He pointed towards the back of the room.

"The city holds onto important documents dating back to 1769 in this part of the library. We have books, periodicals, and microfilms, among other things. You could probably start with the primary documents from the Civil War. We have some collections this way. If you still haven't found what you're looking for, you can always try the microfilm collection."

She nodded, gazing around the expansive space. It was certainly overwhelming. Candy was already roaming around, looking over everyone's shoulder to see what they were working on.

"I can show you where the collection is. Right this way." Walking further into the room, he approached a shelf with several large and old, hardback books, grabbing one and putting it onto the table.

"What do you have there?" she asked as she leaned over to see what the book was about. He moved aside to give her a better view.

"This is a book with all the known casualties from the war. It was a long time ago, so there's an obvious risk his name isn't in here if he was unknown, but I'd imagine that isn't the case if you have heard his name elsewhere. May I ask how you know of him?"

She tried to lick her lips, but her mouth had gone dry. There was no explanation pre-concocted in her head to answer his question and she couldn't tell him the truth. Her chest grew tight as her heart rate rose.

"Tell him he's a long-lost relative. He has no way to know if you're lying," Candy said, having joined the conversation without Hazel realizing she was next to them.

"Oh... um... sorry. He's a long-lost relative I heard about from my grandfather."

He nodded. He seemed to accept her lie. She breathed a sigh of relief. She hated lying, mainly because she was always worried about forgetting the specifics of the lie and getting caught.

"Okay. Well, I hope you find what you're looking for. Please don't hesitate to let me know if you need more help, or you can ask Doris over at that counter." He pointed towards the elderly woman standing at the desk near the entrance of the archives. Unlike the man standing next to her, who looked like he may play jazz on the weekends, Doris looked like a stereotypical librarian. Hazel smiled to herself as the woman pushed her half-moon glasses back up her nose with her finger.

"Thank you so much."

Hazel sat down at the table as he walked away. Candy, having no need to follow the expectations of a living person in the library, hopped on top of the table and sat with her legs crossed in front of her.

"He was cute," she said, still watching the man as he walked away. "So... need any help?" She peered into the book as Hazel opened it.

It was obvious that the book had been created a long time ago, although not as long ago as its content on its pages. It appeared as though someone had made copies of the documents created in the 1800s and bound them into a hardcover book.

She flipped through the book of casualties, looking for the last name of Miller, hoping to find the spirit's name, a task she realized would be more difficult than she had hoped when she went through the names and found no man matching the age she thought him to be, with the last name he told her. Every listing was too old or much too young.

She wondered if she had misheard his name or misjudged his age. Candy still scanned the open page, but Hazel had given up. She wasn't supposed to talk in a library, so talking to a ghost was probably a bad idea. Biting her lip, she wrote a note on a sheet of paper announcing her defeat, and discreetly slid it in front of Candy. Candy leaned over the note, twirling her hair while she read. As she finished, she leaned closer to Hazel.

"Maybe he didn't die in the battle. Maybe he was a prisoner of war."

Hazel's mouth fell open before rising into a tentative smile. She had not thought about prisoners of war, but something about it seemed right. She'd seen visions of the man being trapped in some sort of stone room where he was scared. Maybe that was why she saw that vision. Maybe he wanted her to see the location. Returning pen to paper, she wrote another note to Candy, saying 'you're a genius' before flipping back to the Table of Contents in the book.

A flurry of long crimson hair grazed along her arm as Candy flipped her hair back with a satisfied flourish. "Of course, I am, doll."

Hazel only gave her a second glance before returning her attention to the massive book in front of her. Thankfully, there was a section of the book for the men who were assumed to be prisoners of war. Scanning the names, just as she had before, she looked for a Private Miller, who was in his mid to late twenties.

As soon as the name appeared in front of her, a cold chill raced through her body, and she knew she had found her man. His name was Private Steven Miller. Private Miller went missing after the Union mortar boats entered the mouth of the Mississippi River and attacked Fort Jackson for five days, beginning on April 18, 1862. He had been taken by the North, among thousands of other men, and held as a prisoner of war, where he was expected to have died, although the Confederacy did not have confirmation of his death... but Hazel did.

All she needed to do was find out why he was still around and had not crossed over to where he belonged. It was not an easy feat. She could not even guarantee she would run into him again.

CHAPTER EIGHTEEN

Chance Encounters

Making a copy of the page with Private Miller's information, Hazel set the book back onto its shelf and exited the library. She could do the rest of her research at home.

As soon as they climbed into the car, Candy turned to her with expectant eyes. "So, now that you know a little more about him, do you have any ideas about how he found you?"

Hazel placed the key into the ignition but paused to think about Candy's question, trying to go through all the places she visited in the past week where she could have picked up a new spirit.

"I'm really not sure. In the past week, I went to my office and the courthouse, but I'm not sure why he would have popped up there. Both buildings are old but not Civil War old. Plus, I've worked there for a few months, so I don't know why he would appear now. I definitely didn't pick him up at the store, because I didn't go to any of them." She managed a sad chuckle. Candy rolled her eyes.

"You did use your free ticket to the Insectarium that you got from work, though. Had you ever been there before?"

Hazel raised her eyebrows before pulling her cellphone out of her bag and opening the web browser. "I had not been there before. Let me pull it up and see what I can find out about the building. That's a good idea."

Pulling up the search for the Audubon Insectarium, Hazel saw it was on the first floor of the U.S. Custom House federal building. Going a step further and researching the building itself, she gasped.

"I'll be damned." She stared at the webpage before looking to Candy, who was watching her anxiously.

"What?"

"Listen to this... the building the Insectarium is in was built in 1848! It says that the partially completed building was briefly used by the Union Army after New Orleans was taken over in 1862 to house captured Confederate soldiers. It says they had over two thousand soldiers in there!"

Candy blinked rapidly. "Wow, doll. That's crazy. I had no idea. Should we go there to look for him?"

"I guess it's better than having him appear when I've just gotten out of the shower."

Candy snickered, but the thought of it gave Hazel the creeps. Putting her car into drive, she inched onto the busy street and turned in the Insectarium's direction.

Being in the heart of the French Quarter, Hazel had to drive around the block several times to find a parking spot, which would cost her more than a day's worth of food. She grimaced as she swiped her credit card in the machine to get a parking permit.

Since it was a Sunday, the Insectarium was crawling with people. She wondered, for a moment, if she should have gone on a quieter day when she could have had more privacy with the spirit. Of course, what mattered was whether he would show up at all. Having gone to the Insectarium only a few days prior, Hazel easily remembered her steps to retrace, hoping Private Miller was still haunting the spot where he had first seen her.

Her last stop was inside the small theater, where a comedic film clip played while she sat. There were only a few people inside the space, so she opted to remain once they left, hoping the spirit would find her there. Trying to locate him quicker, she had already sent Candy out into the venue to see if she could find him in spaces where living people could not venture.

She sat quietly for a few minutes, biting her fingernails until they nearly bled, before a drop in the temperature drew her attention. Chills raced across her body as she scanned the small space for Private Miller.

Blending almost into the background, he stood near the entrance of the back room in the theater. Once he caught her eye, he moved through the door and into the room, and was blocked from sight.

She swore under her breath before standing up and trying the door, hoping there were no living people inside. The last thing she wanted was to get caught in a location where she wasn't supposed to be and get kicked out of the Insectarium altogether.

The unlocked door opened into a small control room that was, to her relief, empty. Private Miller stood against the stone wall in the back of the room, red faced and shivering. She approached him gingerly, rolling her feet to silence her footsteps. He watched her nervously, maintaining his silence until she got closer.

"I don't know where I am. Can you help me?"

"I think you died in this building a long time ago. Do you remember what happened to you?"

His spectral form flickered, but he maintained his presence. He shook his head solemnly.

"*Died?*"

A blank expression spread across his face as she thought about how she could explain to him what happened without making him upset, but she didn't think there was an easy way to convince someone they were dead.

Pulling the document copies she made at the library out of her satchel, Hazel sat down on the chair at the desk and spread the paperwork out in front of her.

"I want to show you something," she said. "You can come closer."

Hesitating only for a moment, the spirit of Private Miller moved closer to her, leaning his head over the papers where she was pointing. His face fell as he read until his legs folded into a sitting position. He sat quietly, mulling over the words on the page that confirmed his death.

"Hazel, are you in... Oh." Candy slid in through the door, her voice booming through the quiet space. She quieted once she saw them, but it didn't matter. The soldier's spirit had vanished. Candy flushed as she watched Hazel's face fall into a frown.

"Damn it, Candy. I was trying to wrap this thing up. Now he's gone." She circled her hands in front of her furiously, where the spirit had been.

"I'm sorry, doll. I had no idea he was in here, or that he was so jumpy."

Hazel stood up, throwing her satchel over her shoulder. "Whatever. Let's go home."

Walking back to her car, Hazel felt mentally and physically numb. She had been hopeful she would be able to solve the mystery, satisfy the spirit enough to make him cross over, and be home in time to order takeout. But that possibility had been dashed by Candy's unexpected entrance into the back room of the theater.

After a brief stint in traffic, Hazel and Candy arrived back at the apartment, fast food burger in hand. Having to work the next day, Hazel ate her food and then climbed into the shower so she could get to bed at a decent hour, not that her insomnia wouldn't keep her up, anyway. Her mornings at the courthouse were early and stressful, so she didn't enjoy going in under-slept.

Getting into bed that night, her mind was unsettled. She hated being so close to a resolution and then having to leave it unresolved. It weighed on her. At some point, after hours of tossing and turning, unconsciousness overtook her.

CHAPTER NINETEEN

Freedom, Alas

"Where's your superior, Private?" A middle-aged man with a thick black beard loomed over me, every muscle in his face tense. I squeezed my mouth shut, refusing to speak.

Forcing a burlap bag onto my head, they pushed me back down as a deluge of water poured over my face, bursting through my clenched jaw and flooding into my nose. I coughed and spluttered as the water replaced air. I was taught to be a strong man, but the sobs won their way through my will.

"Your superior," he demanded. "Where is he?"

I cried violently. I genuinely didn't know the answer. Shaking my head frantically, my breaths came in rapid bursts. "I don't know!"

Sounds of a musket being loaded echoed from somewhere in the room. Fear clouded my vision.

"I'm going to ask you one more time, boy. Where are they?"

"I don't know," I sobbed.

A shot rang out before pain flooded into my leg, and everything turned black.

Waking from a startling nightmare, Hazel choked on nothing, still feeling the water flooding into her mouth from the vision that wasn't hers. Her heart raced, making her feel lightheaded. The bedroom was dark, but a patch of the darkness was blacker than the rest. She squinted against the darkness, trying to understand the shapes.

"Candy... is that you?"

There was no answer. The dark figure moved closer, only slightly.

Reaching a trembling hand to the lamp next to her bed, she flicked the switch on, squinting her eyes against the instant brightness. The spectral body of Private Miller flickered near the foot of her bed. He held his cap in his hands against his chest.

"Private Miller," she gasped. "You scared me."

"I'm sorry, ma'am. I just wanted to tell you thank you."

Hazel blinked and then bit her lip. She didn't know what he could possibly want to thank her for.

"I'm sorry... I just don't understand. I wasn't able to do anything to help you."

He moved closer to sit on the bed. She instinctively flinched but his eyes held a warmth she had not seen before.

"You did, though. I woke up, and I didn't know how I had gotten there... I didn't know why I was there. I needed help to understand what was happening, and you showed me. No one else could see me. They couldn't answer my pleas. But you did. I think, maybe, that I thought I was still stuck there. I followed you here, but I didn't recognize this world. It wasn't the place I had seen before my sleep. Now I understand..." He looked behind himself, at something Hazel could not see, before returning his eyes to her. They were glassy, but hopeful. "I'm ready to go home."

A warmth filled Hazel's heart when his words met her ears. He was ready to go home. The resolution had found its way to him. She nodded, reaching out her hand to lay it against his arm.

The iciness of his body chilled her, but she held her shivers at bay. "I'm so glad you are ready to go to a better place. I only wish this could have come to you sooner. I'm sorry it took so long."

Patting her hand with his, he rose from the bed, smiled, and vanished. Her hand was resting upon her own arm when Candy floated in through the doorway.

"Hey, you awake?"

Hazel shot her a sideways glance before flopping back onto the bed.

"Candy... If we are going to make it as roommates, we really will need to come out with a system for you to knock before entering. You nearly scared him away again."

Candy flopped down next to her, long, red hair tickling the side of Hazel's face.

"We'll figure something out, doll. At least before you start having sex with Tate. It would be a shame if I saw him naked or something."

Rolling her eyes, Hazel sighed before turning over in her bed and pulling her blanket up to her chin. "Good night, Casper."

"Good night, roomie."

To be continued...

Afterword

If you enjoyed this book, don't forget to leave a review! Reviews are vital to authors! They help books reach new readers. I really appreciate it!

https://www.amazon.com/dp/B09LVT559K

SAVING SCARLETT

Sample

C.A. VARIAN

Chapter 1

THE SURVIVOR

"Scar, wake up."

Hearing my friend Ashley's voice, my eyes fluttered open, my neck cramping as I tried to lift my head. The chair beneath me was not fit for sleeping. "What time is it?"

Not answering right away, she moved across my office and opened the shades, the sun nearly blinding me. "It's eight in the morning. Damn, Scar. Did you stay here all night?"

"Huh? Eight..." My words trailed off as I got ahold of my senses. There was a reason I'd slept at my bookstore, Tangled in the Pages, but not one I was willing to share, not even with her. "I worked late trying to get inventory done and food prep for the store before morning shift, but I hadn't intended to sleep here."

Shaking her head, Ashley placed a cup of coffee in my hand. "Do you want to go home and change? Maybe put some ice on that. How in the hell did you do that to yourself?"

When she pointed at my face, I lost all ability to breathe, my lungs seizing as images of what had happened the day before flooded into my head—the beating he'd given me—again. I lifted my fingers to my cheek, touching the area where my eye was swollen. Grinning, I feigned embarrassment. No one knew my shameful secret. "Oh. Yeah. I took a book to the eye last night. I must not have pushed it all the way onto the shelf."

Ashley turned a side eye in my direction. "You know I'll help you with inventory. All you have to do is ask. Especially since you seem to keep getting more and more clumsy these days. How old are you again? Eighty?"

Huffing a laugh, I took a deep sip of the coffee, closing my eyes as it fed my caffeine addiction. "I'm thirty and I was just tired. That's what I get for working so late every night, but I can't seem to help myself. This place is my dream, after all."

While I dug in my purse for headache medication, she left my office and began working on the opening procedures.

Once Ashley put the money into the register, she returned to me, looking more closely at my injury. I hissed as she touched it, even though her hand was gentle.

"You may need to have that looked at in case you have a concussion. And go home at night, Scar. Work can wait until the next morning."

I grinned and nodded. There was so much I wanted to tell my friend but couldn't, or at least, *wouldn't*. "I'll go home and take a shower. Are you sure you'll be okay while I'm gone? Can I bring you back something to eat?"

With a shake of her head, she all but shoved me toward the door. "We have pastries here. I'll be fine. Now go and get yourself presentable and put on lots of concealer."

When I got in my car, I checked my phone and was relieved to have no messages. My husband, Joshua, knew I was at the store and had not called to check up on me. I wasn't surprised. He'd probably gone straight to his mistress the moment I'd left the house. All I hoped was that he wasn't home when I got there.

Sucking in a breath as my reality threatened to pour fresh tears out of my bruised eye, I turned up the radio, hoping the music could drown out the thoughts running through my head, all of them telling me to run away.

Since no one was home when I arrived at my house, I took a quick shower and packed an overnight bag, just in case I fell asleep in my bookstore again. It didn't have a bed, but it was still a safe place where I could hide out when I needed to.

By the time I made it back to Tangled in the Pages, my bookstore and coffee shop combo was in full swing. Ashley was taking orders while another employee, Jack, was preparing the food and drinks. Ashley looked up at me as the bell jingled over the door, her eyes telling me they were swamped and needed help. It was the exact reason I had been hesitant to leave in the first place.

Tossing my bags in my office and locking the door, I returned to the front of the store and took over register duty so Ashley could help Jack. With the holidays coming, it was our busiest time of year, which made me wonder if I needed to hire a few more employees to help during the rushes. I'd only had the store for a few years, so it was still a new adventure for me.

I moved to the counter, pouring fresh coffee and greeting customers with practiced ease. The familiar routine calmed my frayed nerves, allowing me to push aside the lingering fear and anxiety. I was safe there in my space, surrounded by the things and people I loved.

"The usual?" I asked an older gentleman, Henry, who came in every morning. He nodded, eyes crinkling behind wire-rimmed glasses.

"You're a lifesaver, cher." His voice was warm, full of affection. "Don't know what I'd do without my morning coffee and chat."

"You'd find another coffee shop," I teased, sliding his coffee across the counter and waving away his attempt to pay. "On the house today, Henry. You deserve it."

"Well, aren't you a sweetheart." Smile deepening, he patted my hand before moving to the chair by the window and burying himself in the newspaper I always set aside for him.

Bumping my shoulder, Ashley nodded at the few customers waiting to be served. "You okay?"

"Yeah." I drew in a steadying breath, meeting her concerned gaze. "I'm okay. Just tired."

"I'm here if you need anything." Her brown eyes were warm, full of affection. She'd been with me since the beginning. "Always."

"I know." I smiled, small but genuinely. "Thank you. For everything."

Smiling, she nudged me again. "Anytime. Now come on, time to get back to work!"

I laughed, following her lead as we set about serving the new customers who'd lined up at the register. With the warmth of an environment I created myself, the familiar routine eased the lingering ache in my chest.

Once the morning rush had calmed, I wiped the dust from the shelves and straightened the stacks of books, admiring my cozy bookstore. The aroma of fresh coffee wafted through the air, mingling with the soft jazz music playing over the speakers. Even if I hadn't owned the store, I realized I would probably spend all my time there. It was the exact way I wanted my customers to feel.

My muscles ached from unloading inventory for hours the night before, but a familiar peace settled over me. My bookstore was my sanctuary, a refuge from a world that had been cruel and unforgiving for too long.

As I bustled around the space, a young couple lounged on the sofa near the fireplace, sipping lattes and reading from well-worn paperbacks. The fireplace didn't get much use, since it was hot as Hades in Louisiana most of the year, but it was still a beautiful feature of the building. Two teenage girls giggled over their cinnamon rolls at a table near the front window and an older man tapped away on his laptop in the corner, a half-empty mug of Earl Grey tea beside him. *My regulars.* They came for the atmosphere as much as for the books and coffee.

Leaning against the counter, I breathed in the familiar scents, feeling tension ease from my shoulders. My gaze wandered to the worn wooden floors and shelves lining the walls, filled with stories of adventure, heartbreak and hope. There were so many lives and worlds contained within the pages to get lost in. I only wished I had more time to read.

A smile tugged at my lips as another wave of customers trickled through the door. My perfect, imperfect world. The one I had built from nothing.

This was *my* story.

My happily ever after.

Joshua *couldn't* take that away from me.

Noticing that a group of college kids had left a stack of books on a small table near the back of the store, which was a daily occurrence, I scooped them up, intending to put them away. I had just started returning them to the shelves when the bell above the door chimed, drawing my gaze. A man stepped inside, tall and broad-shouldered, clad in black from head to toe. Jet black hair fell over piercing blue eyes as he paused just inside the entrance, scanning the room. His gaze was sharp, intense, taking in everything and missing nothing.

Unease flickered through me at his imposing presence, at odds with the cozy atmosphere of my shop. And yet...curiosity stirred as I studied him from beneath my lashes. There was a hardness to his expression, as if he had seen and endured far too much in his life, although he couldn't have been much older than me. But something about his lingering gaze and the way one corner of his mouth tilted upward tugged at my interest and I had to admit, he was sexy as hell.

A mystery waiting to be solved.

His gaze landed on a shelf of tattered paperbacks along the far wall and the hint of a smile softened his angular features. My heart skipped as he strode forward, boots thudding against the wooden floor, and slid out a worn copy of *Treasure Island*.

Interest sparked in those fathomless light blue eyes as he flipped through the pages, as if transported to another time and place. A place of adventure and danger and...*longing*.

Heat crept into my cheeks. I was reading too much into a simple glance and smile, letting my imagination run wild. The stranger was just a customer, here to browse the shelves like any other.

Surprising even myself, I moved across the room, my hands smoothing the front of my apron as I stepped forward to greet him.

I cleared my throat, my pulse quickening like I was an unpopular schoolgirl asking the popular guy to prom. "Find anything interesting?"

Glancing up from the book, a flicker of surprise crossed his expression, as if he hadn't expected me to approach. Still, his lips curved into a slow, devastating smile that did dangerous things to my heart.

"A childhood favorite." As though fate only meant to be crueler, his voice was as smooth and dark as aged whiskey. He held up the book. "*Treasure Island* ignited my love for adventure at a young age."

"Mine as well." I leaned a hip against the shelf, hoping I appeared more at ease than I felt. Inside, my body was buzzing. "The pirates, the danger, the thrill of discovering treasure. Stevenson was a master storyteller."

"That he was." Sliding the book back into place, he turned to face me fully, arms loosely crossing over his chest. Even with my heels, I had to tilt my head back to meet his gaze. "You have an interesting collection here. Not what one would expect in a small coffee shop."

"I'm glad you think so." Although I shrugged, a flush of pride rushed through me. "Books have always been my passion. There's nothing quite like getting lost in a good story, discovering new worlds and characters."

"An escape from reality." His tone had gone pensive, as if he understood that need on a deeper level. "And a glimpse into the lives of others, to remind us we're not alone."

I stared at him, struck by the insight. He saw it, the power of stories—of words—to transcend our circumstances and forge connections.

A slow smile curved my lips. "It seems we have more in common than a love for *Treasure Island*, Mr...?"

As if realizing he hadn't introduced himself, he blinked, the way his thick dark lashes framed his blue eyes only making him more handsome. "Bane."

Our gazes held for a long moment, a strange tension simmering between us. I couldn't look away from his eyes, pale blue and piercing, and I realized at that moment that his name was an omen. Something told me this man could destroy me and I would love every second of it.

Reminding myself that I was indeed married and that I shouldn't think such things, I licked my dry lips, all too aware of my heartbeat quickening.

"Bane," I repeated. Even as I was berating myself for the awkward response, one corner of his mouth lifted in a half-smile that nearly threw my equilibrium off balance. "It's a pleasure."

"The pleasure is mine...?" He posed it as a question, obviously waiting for my name.

"I'm Scarlett."

Bane's gaze dipped to my mouth and then lower, a slow perusal that had heat pooling low in my belly. I shifted on my feet, torn between embarrassment at my reaction and a reckless urge to move closer to him, to close the space between us.

When his eyes returned to mine, a knowing glint lit their depths. As if he sensed the effect he had on me. As if he relished it. I didn't doubt he had that effect on all the ladies, and for reasons I didn't dare question, I was slightly jealous about that.

A blush stained my cheeks and I took a step back, breaking the spell. "Well," I said, a bit breathless, "let me know if you need any more book recommendations. I'm always here."

"I'll be sure to do that." Amusement lurked in his tone and he gave a slight bow of his head. "It was a pleasure meeting you, Scarlett."

Saving me from embarrassing myself any further, the bell above the door jingled, telling me new customers had entered the store. I smiled at him once more before turning to look back toward the counter, my hands twisting in my apron.

"That's my cue, but if you come to the register, I would be happy to give you a cup of coffee—on the house, of course. Since you have such good taste in books."

Chapter 2

THE SAVIOR

The moonlight glinted off the blade of my favorite knife as I crept through the shadows toward my target. My footsteps were silent, my breathing steady. I was in my element.

Pausing behind a pillar, my eyes scanned the lavish ballroom before they fell on Auguste LaRoche, the corrupt businessman who had made far too many enemies. His receding hairline did nothing to hide the look of smug entitlement on his face as he laughed loudly with a group of partygoers. Little did he know those would be the last laughs he ever shared. Moving away from the group, he lifted his whiskey to his mouth, watching his guests.

I adjusted my grip on the knife, the leather of my gloves creaking ever so slightly. LaRoche's personal bodyguards stood several feet away, oblivious to the predator in their midst. *Fools.* Their complacency would cost their boss his life.

In one swift movement, I slipped behind LaRoche and pressed the cold steel to his throat, pulling him behind the pillar with me. His laughter transformed into a strangled gasp. The bodyguards whirled around, hands flying to their hip holsters, but they were too late. I'd already pulled him into a back hallway—out of sight.

"Please, I'll give you anything. Just don't—"

His begging turned into a gurgle as I slashed the knife across his throat, scarlet spilling down his white tuxedo shirt as he collapsed onto the white marble floor. As chaos erupted in the ballroom a moment later when his guards undoubtedly found him, I was already gone, disappearing into the night.

Another contract was completed. It was another day my niece would live to see, thanks to the funds from the night's kill. For her, I would paint the world red. For her, I would be a monster.

The sterile scent of antiseptic hit my nose as I walked through the automatic doors of the hospital. So late at night, the lights in the hallways were dimmed, the bustling crowds of the daytime replaced by the soft footsteps of nurses on night shift. I made my way to the pediatric intensive care unit, the one place in this world that made my chest constrict with emotion. It was past visiting hours, but no one ever stopped me from entering when I showed up. My money paid for part of their salary.

I nodded to the nurse at the desk before continuing to room four hundred and twenty-eight—Evelyn's room. Pushing the door open with a gentle hand, my eyes landed on my seven-year-old niece's tiny body lying motionless in the bed, the steady beep of the heart monitor the only indication she still clung to life. Her skin was pale, her bald head covered by a pink knitted cap.

Dark circles stood out under her closed eyes, eyes that should have been filled with joy and laughter rather than pain.

Pulling a chair up next to her bed, I took her tiny hand in mine. So delicate, so fragile. Hard to believe that little hand once felt strong enough to grab onto my fingers as I swung her around the yard.

"Hey kiddo," I whispered. "I'm back."

No response, not that I expected one. The experimental treatment kept her unconscious most days, her body too weak to face the world. But I knew on some level she could sense I was there.

"I did it. I got the money for your next treatment." My voice caught, wishing I could take away her pain. "So, you just hang in there. You're going to get better soon, I promise."

Bringing her hand up to my lips, I kissed it before setting it back down. I had to believe she would recover. The alternative was too agonizing to face.

"I love you, Evie. Be strong for me."

I sat with her a while longer, keeping a silent vigil over her fragile form. For her, I would walk through the fires of hell. For her, I would make sure she survived—no matter the cost.

The door opened and I turned to see my sister entering, her black hair pulled back into a messy bun. Dark circles stood out under her eyes as well, a testament to the many sleepless nights she'd spent at Evelyn's bedside.

Sitting beside me, Caroline placed a delicate hand on my shoulder. "She's fighting hard. Our girl's a warrior."

I nodded, a lump forming in my throat. Evelyn was the strongest person I knew, enduring endless treatments and pain with seldom a complaint. She inherited her strength from her mother, who was practically a superhero. Ever since Daniel, my sister's husband, had been tragically killed in a car crash, I'd been doing everything in my power to take care of them, but they took care of me, too. We were the only family we had left, and I would have done anything for them.

Tapping the white, two-by-three piece of cardstock in my hand, I listened as the stiff-shirt CEO across from me droned on about the hit he wanted to take out on his unsuspecting wife and exactly how he wanted it done. Killing was my thing. It was the one thing I was really fucking good at, and I didn't need this asshole telling me how to do my job. Still, I didn't interrupt him. The more he spoke, the redder his face became, and I secretly hoped he would have a heart attack and keel over in his chair. I already had his payment in my pocket, a stack of unmarked bills that he wasn't getting back, even if he did croak in front of me.

Whenever I met with a potential client for the first time, I always tried to come up with their story in my headfirst just to see how close I was—just to see how good I was at reading people. This guy was easy, no matter how hard he tried to convince me otherwise. He wanted to convince me that his wife was evil incarnate, the devil in disguise, but it all came down to greed. That's all it ever was for these white-collar assholes looking for a hit on their spouses.

From what I gathered, he wanted her out of the way, but he wanted to keep all the money. Simply put, his mistress was pregnant, and he wanted to marry her. Out with the old and in with the new. He knew if his wife found out, she would take him for all he was worth, but if she died... If his wife died in any way other than suicide, he would make a killing on her life insurance. *Pun intended*. Then, he would be able to marry his current mistress and find a new side piece as well. In other words, he would be able to move on with his life by repeating the cycle.

I could make it look like an accident or even a home robbery, and I wasn't there to question *why* he wanted her dead. There was no reason for him to tell me half of the shit that came tumbling out of his mouth. In my line of work, I tried to stay away from all that. I didn't care why someone ordered a hit or whether the target was a modern-day saint. My job was simple: take out the target and make money. Period. Whether his wife was the devil or the sweetest woman on the planet, I didn't give a shit. What he really needed was a therapist to talk to, even his barber would do, someone he could ramble to for a few hours to make him feel important. I had better things to do.

The underground club we sat in was a shady place in downtown New Orleans, but I'd chosen it specifically because I knew no one inside would speak a word of our meeting. Even though I didn't own the club, and the owner didn't even know my real name, he was indebted to me for a big job I'd done for him in the past. As far as the other patrons, most of them were so strung out that they wouldn't even remember being there themselves by the time they woke up in the morning, if they woke up at all.

As the clock ticked, I looked at my phone, pretending to get a message so he would get the hint that he needed to stop talking. "All I need to know is a general timeline and where to find her. I have to go, so if that's all..."

I pushed back in my chair, standing to leave, when he slid a slip of paper across the table. "This is my address. I'll be out of town next week at a business conference. She should be home alone then."

Thinking he was done speaking, *finally*, I turned to walk away when he grabbed my wrist.

I came very close to knocking him unconscious for touching me, but I clenched my jaw and turned back to look at him. "Don't ever put your hands on me," I growled, pulling out of his grip. "Not if you want to keep them."

Knowing what was good for him, he backed away, holding his hands up in supplication. "I'm sorry. I'm sorry. I just wanted to add the code to our security system so you can get inside the house."

Annoyance still boiling in my blood, I handed the paper back to him, scanning the club again as he scribbled some digits onto it. We'd been in there for way too long. I never let my meetings go on for that long, and I should have shut him down twenty minutes earlier, but I was amusing myself with how talking about his wife turned his face the color of a firetruck.

The moment he held the paper back out to me, I yanked it out of his hand, and walked away.

Slipping the paper into my pocket, I walked out of the bar and back into the alley.

As I strolled toward my downtown apartment, I couldn't help but chuckle. How big of an idiot was he to give the security code to get into his home to a known killer? It was then that I decided that I would definitely pay them a visit—*before* he left for his trip. Since I had the keys to the castle, I may as well have a little bit of fun.

Chapter 3

THE SURVIVOR

The closer I got to home, the tighter my chest became, threatening to squeeze out the air in my lungs. Although I knew it was stupid to return home, and that some would blame me for the bruises on my skin barely camouflaged by expensive makeup, leaving Joshua wasn't as simple as it seemed. Everything I had was tied to my husband's business. Our home. Our money. My business. Everything. Even if I were willing to throw it all away, the threats—and his connections—kept me at home. They made it impossible for me to escape him. Since my husband was more concerned about his public image than he was about me, he would not be willing to face the embarrassment of me leaving him. I was trapped in a life I didn't want and powerless to change it. The feeling that I had no control over my life and was completely powerless over it was overwhelming for me, but I didn't know what else to do.

Bane, the man who'd talked to me about the adventures of *Treasure Island* that morning, had never come to the register for his coffee. He must have slipped out when I returned behind the counter to fix it for him. It occupied my thoughts for the rest of the day. I couldn't fathom why he left a perfectly tasty, free cup of coffee on the counter. Even though I was married, I couldn't get him out of my mind, and it was troubling. His eyes had captivated me and held me in place until I didn't know which direction I was going. The fact that I would probably never see him again was for the best but fantasizing about him wasn't a bad thing. In a life overshadowed with darkness, the thought of the handsome stranger could bring in a little light.

The interstate traffic crawled along at a glacial place as I made my way through downtown, my mind keeping me occupied the entire time. The New Orleans freeways had been undergoing road construction for at least two decades, and I could see no end in sight. Even though I had left shortly after my store closed, the time of day didn't matter. There was always traffic.

Blowing out a breath, I pressed the key fob button to open the gate into my neighborhood, hoping my husband wasn't home. In the event he wasn't there, I could only speculate where he was, but anywhere was better than at home with me. I wasn't certain he had a mistress, but I wsasn't naive either. A huge part of me hoped he had someone else. I hoped one day he would leave me for her, so I could move on with my life. Perhaps one day I would be able to build a family and experience true love. Until then, my secret IUD would remain in place. In no way would I bring a child into a loveless marriage. If I did, I would never be able to escape.

The night sky was dark when I pulled into the driveway, the lights of the city blotting out the stars. It was like as a visual representation of my life, the light in me nearly snuffed out by the constant barrage of suffering.

While the engine was still running, I sat in my car for a moment, not opening the garage door right away. If my husband was home, he would demand to know why I hadn't returned home the night before, and no excuse would suffice. He would accuse me of cheating, as he always did, and then we would fight all night long. Despite my better judgment, I had never cheated. I had never given myself the chance to feel pleasure without pain, but that didn't matter. He was a narcissist, a master of gaslighting, and I couldn't even remember how or when exactly he became that way. It was impossible for me to pinpoint the moment when my love had turned into a monster. He hadn't always been like that, but perhaps I had been so blinded by the good times that I had ignored all the warning signs. In any case, it didn't matter anymore. There was a lot I wished I could do over, but time only moved in one direction.

Swallowing down the fear that bubbled in my throat, I pressed the button to open my garage door. The moment I noticed my husband standing where I usually parked, with a glass of whiskey in his hand, my heart sank. His expression gave no indication of his mood, so I could not tell whether he was angry. Blood roared in my ears as my heart beat violently, my fight-or-flight instincts telling me to turn around and drive away. Still, I smiled at him—faked the happiest smile I could—as I slowly inched my vehicle into my space when he moved out of the way.

As soon as I shifted the car into park, he grabbed me by the arm and yanked me out of the car. One arm still ensnared in the seatbelt, I hit the concrete floor with a heavy thud. My hip and back exploded with pain just as the liquor glass hit the ground beside me, covering me with tiny glass shards. I cried out, tears burning the backs of my eyes, but he didn't give me a chance to process what was happening before he yanked me up by my shoulders and threw me up against the side of my car.

"Where the hell were you last night, Scarlett?" His voice was filled with vitriol, and the smell of whiskey on his breath nearly made me vomit. I tried to slow my breathing even as my body screamed in pain, but I knew he could see the fear in my eyes. I was nothing more than prey, a scared animal trapped in a cage.

"Josh, please calm down. While doing inventory at the bookstore, I fell asleep. It was—"

Surging forward, he grabbed my arm, his fingers digging into my flesh. "When I come home, I expect a hot meal waiting for me. Do you understand?"

I nodded, blinking back tears as I slid out of his grip and scurried into the house. Keeping my eyes downcast, I pulled leftovers out of the freezer, busying my hands preparing dinner. The kitchen was spotless, not a dish out of place. I had learned the hard way that a messy house only fueled Joshua's anger.

As I finished plating his food and set his plate on the table, my hands trembled. I stood motionless, watching him eat. My appetite was nonexistent.

After only a few bites, he slammed his fork down. "This chicken is dry. Can't you do anything right?"

Before I could respond, he grabbed the plate and flung it at me. I barely had time to duck as it shattered against the wall, shards of porcelain raining down around me as he rose from his chair.

"Useless bitch."

I scrambled backwards across the floor as he advanced, my back hitting the wall as he towered over me, his face contorted in rage. Curling into a ball, my arms did their best to shield my head when the first blow fell.

Over and over, his boot connected with my ribs, his fists punching me as I cried out in pain and pleaded for him to stop. After what felt like an eternity, he finally stepped back, breathing heavily.

"Clean up this mess," he spat, stalking out of the house. Only a second later, I heard him speed away, a sob of relief breaking free the moment he did.

Every inch of my body screamed in agony as I struggled to my hands and knees. I wanted to lie there and sob, but I knew better. Move, I told myself. *Survive.* This was not the first beating I had endured at Joshua's hands, and it likely wouldn't be the last. I refused to let him break me, but I couldn't leave. I couldn't even walk. For a moment, I just needed rest.

I dragged myself upstairs to my bathroom, barely able to stand. Leaning against the sink, I avoided my reflection in the mirror. I didn't need to see the damage to know it was bad. My ribs throbbed with every breath. When I lifted my shirt, dark bruises were already forming across my torso. My lip was split and bleeding, and my right eye was almost swollen shut.

Climbing into my bed, I finally allowed the tears to fall as I waited for the darkness to consume me and take the pain away.

Want to see what happens next?
Finding Saving Scarlett, including
two gorgeous special editions, at
https://cavarian.com/saving-scarlett

Also By

Hazel Watson Mystery Series

Kindred Spirits: Prequel

The Sapphire Necklace

Justice for the Slain

Whispers from the Swamp

Crossroads of Death

The Spirit Collector (coming October 2023)

Crown of the Phoenix Series

Crown of the Phoenix

Crown of the Exiled

Crown of the Prophecy (Coming Soon)

Mate of the Phoenix

Supernatural Savior Series

Song of Death

Goddess of Death

An Other World Series

The Other World

The Other Key

The Other Fate (coming January 2024)

My Alien Mate Series

My Alien Protector

Acknowledgements

I want to thank my editor, Megan, of Willow Oak Author Services for putting up with my crazy editing schedule. (At least I keep the work coming).

I would like to thank Blurbs, Baubles, and Book Covers for this book's amazing cover.

My final thank you is to my family, friends, and most of all, my readers.

Thank you for your support!

Follow C.A. Varian

Sign up for C. A. Varian's newsletter to receive current updates on her new and upcoming releases, sales, and giveaways:

You can also find all stories, books, and social media pages and follow her here:

https://linktr.ee/cavarian

https://cavarian.com/

About the Author

Raised in a small town in the heart of Louisiana's Cajun Country, C. A. Varian spent most of her childhood fishing, crabbing, and getting sunburnt at the beach. Her love of reading began very young, and she would often compete at school to read enough books to earn prizes.

Graduating with the first of her college degrees as a mother of two in her late twenties, she became a public-school teacher, which is the career she still held until June 1, 2023, when she became a fulltime author!

Writing became a passion project, and she put out her first novel in 2021, and has continued to publish new novels every few months since then, not slowing down for even a minute.

Married to a retired military officer, she spent many years moving around for his career, but they now live in central Alabama, with her youngest daughter, Arianna. Her oldest daughter, Brianna, is enjoying her happily ever after with her new husband and several pups. C. A. Varian has two Shih Tzus that she considers her children. Boy, Charlie, and girl, Luna, are their mommy's shadows. She also has three cats named Ramses, Simba, and Cookie.

9 781961 238244